STELLA AND THE FIRESHIPS

By the same author:

Mutiny in the Caribbean
The Malta Frigate
Seven Gun Broadside
The Quarterdeck Ladder

Stella and the Fireships

SHOWELL STYLES

WILLIAM KIMBER · LONDON

First published in 1985 by
WILLIAM KIMBER & CO. LIMITED
100 Jermyn Street, London SW1Y 6EE

ISBN 0-7183-0581-7

Photoset in North Wales by
Derek Doyle & Associates Mold, Clwyd
and printed in Great Britain by
Biddles Limited, Guildford, Surrey

Contents

All the chief characters in this
book (including Stella) really
existed. All the chief events
really took place.

I

Stella

1

Stella was born at half-past five in the morning of 26th October 1800. At this moment of time, three bells in the morning watch, two of the three persons with whose lives her own was to be curiously entwined were asleep: Captain Lord Cochrane in his cabin on board the sloop *Speedy*, Miss Katherine Corbett Barnes in her attic bedroom in London. The third person, Lieutenant William Bissell, was lying flat on his back on the deck of a French brig with a French knife an inch from his throat.

This predicament of Mr Bissell had originated six hours earlier in the stern-cabin of His Majesty's ship *Montagu* of 74 guns.

Captain Knight was sitting behind his table in the big cabin, which was filled with the muted noises of the big ship's steady rush through a wind-whipped sea. He swept a quick glance across the faces of the four officers standing in front of him with their cocked hats tucked under their arms. They all stood lopsidedly, left leg bent and right leg straight, because *Montagu* was laid on the starboard tack in a stiff breeze and the cabin deck sloped considerably to port. The shifting light of the two bulkhead lamps in their gimbals showed a row of intent weather-browned features.

'Cutter and longboat,' said the captain; he was small and square-jawed with a clipped utterance. 'Mr Bissell and Mr

Knott in the cutter, Mr Alexander and Mr Mitchell in the longboat. Mr Bissell commands. No firearms to be taken, Mr Bissell.'

'Aye aye, sir,' said Bissell in a voice both deep and harsh.

Montagu's second lieutenant was tall and angular, with a high-bridged nose and somewhat prominent blue eyes which gave him a perpetually defiant look and made him appear younger than his thirty-one years.

'You've all seen how the brig lies,' continued Captain Knight. 'Snug enough under the Port Louis batteries. Shoals north of the entrance, La Haie rocks south. A couple of miles of sea-room. Anchors fore and aft, no doubt.'

'She has two out for'ard, sir, by your leave,' said Bissell. 'I made them out with my glass, from the foremast-head this afternoon.'

Knight's grizzled brows drew together in momentary irritation. 'Then you'll naturally detail two axemen to cut them. The cutting-out should present no difficulty. You'll board from either side –' He caught himself up, with a brief smile. 'But I've no need to teach you gentlemen your duty in such a business. Cutting-out an enemy vessel must be nigh on second nature to you.'

Three of his four officers grinned and nodded respectfully; since she had been detached from Collingwood's blockading fleet for an independent cruise *Montagu* had taken or burned twenty-seven French merchant-ships. Lieutenant Bissell nodded but his bony face remained serious.

'So it's boats away at six bells, morning watch,' Knight went on. 'Half-an-hour should find you alongside with this onshore wind, and there'll be light enough for you to bring her out. No lights, no alarm if you can manage it, and you'll have her clear before the batteries open fire. I shall stand in to reply if they do. And that's all. Any questions, gentlemen?' He frowned as his ranging glance rested on Bissell, who was plainly about to speak. 'Well, Mr Bissell?'

'Well, sir,' said Bissell, raising his chin a trifle, 'I'd like to suggest – by your leave, sir, that is – to suggest an alternative course. The wind –'

'Not,' said Knight forcibly between his teeth, 'not fireships again, I trust?'

'You could use the *Marie Payot*, sir – she's the least valuable of the prizes.' Bissell, leaning forward in his eagerness, spoke swift and loud. 'We've ample combustibles and conditions are ideal. If this wind were to shift another point west we could even dispense with fireship's boat and crew. It's a moral certainty the brig cuts her cables even if the fireship heads wide of her, and she's on a lee shore. I could see the breakers on the rocks. She'd be a total wreck –'

'Thank you, Mr Bissell!' The captain slapped the table angrily with his hand. 'Making every allowance for what we've come to know as the bee in your bonnet, I must remind you that my orders are given and that you will obey them.'

'Aye aye, sir,' said Bissell woodenly.

If he resented a near-reprimand delivered in front of officers junior to himself he contrived to conceal it. Knight's irritable glare removed itself at the sound of a throat being cleared.

'Well, Mr Knott?'

Knott, fourth lieutenant, was a stocky middle-aged man whose voice, in contrast to Bissell's, was a diffident mumble. He was sharply bidden to speak up.

'Begging your pardon, sir,' muttered Knott, recommencing, 'the master reckons this wind'll strengthen and shift westerly before dawn. That being so, and tide making an hour after low water, the brig might well find it – humph – difficult to beat out against it.'

'And the master might well be wrong,' retorted the captain. 'Mr Knott, I want that brig. She's a fine big vessel and she'll be carrying a valuable cargo. You reported her deep-laden, Mr Bissell, I fancy?'

'So far as I could see, sir, she appeared deep-laden,' Bissell said cautiously.

'If you could see her two bow cables you could see that, I should hope. What is it, Mr Knott?'

'Just a thought, sir,' Knott mumbled apologetically. 'Deep-laden, she'll be the more awkward to handle, bringing her out.'

'You and Bissell seem intent on finding difficulties!' Knight exploded. 'It's not what I expect –'

He checked himself and pursed his lips, considering what had been said; he was a fair-minded man, and these two officers were experienced seamen.

'What's your course out of Port Louis?' he shot at Bissell.

'West by north, sir.'

'Very well. Should the wind strengthen and veer to west by north – and I don't think it will, mark you – it's like enough the brig would fail to pass the entrance. In that case, Mr Bissell, you may set fire to her. I must rely, as you see,' he added acidly, 'upon your judgement of wind force and direction.'

'Aye aye, sir,' said Bissell stolidly.

'Very well, then. Further questions? Mr Alexander? Mr Mitchell?' Captain Knight stood up. 'You'll please to muster your boat-crews in good time, gentlemen.'

They filed out past the marine sentry into the windy darkness of the after-deck. Overhead on the quarterdeck Taplin, the first lieutenant, was bellowing orders and they had to dodge the dark figures of the watch-on-deck running to take a haul on the sheets. *Montagu*, under main courses and topsails, was snoring along through the night sea, retrieving the sea-miles lost that afternoon when she had passed within sight of Port Louis and held on westward – for Ushant and the Channel, as the French (Captain Knight hoped) would think. Alexander, fourth lieutenant, and Mitchell, acting-lieutenant and master's mate, had disappeared for'ard. Bissell gripped Knott's elbow.

'My cabin,' he said shortly, and they groped their way down to the second lieutenant's dark hutch below the wardroom. 'Got to let off steam,' he explained when they were sitting on his seachest with their heads together; it was a phrase he had learned from Knott, whose uncle was overseer in the Royal Laboratory at Woolwich.

'Go ahead,' Knott grunted.

He was nine years older than Bissell but junior to him because Bissell's commission bore an earlier date. This had not prevented the development of friendship between the two.

'Foolery,' said Bissell, blowing out his breath on the word. 'Waste. Unnecessary risk. Stick to the old ways at any cost. What are we here for, Knott? To destroy enemy shipping and create fear and dismay along the French coasts. What could do that better than a fireship?'

'He wants a prize,' muttered Knott.

'Aye – prize-money. God damn prize-money! Our business is to smash French ships, not take 'em away to market. See here, Knott.' Bissell's voice sharpened. 'If there's a head-wind – and it'll veer, that's a moral certainty – we can't bring her out. What then? We fire her and pull back. The blaze alerts the batteries before we're half-a-cable clear. Ship and boats at risk, and all because Knight chooses to gamble on getting a few more pounds into his pocket.'

Knott shifted uneasily on the sea-chest. 'Keep your voice down, Will,' he growled. 'That's court-martial talk.'

'And you've heard it all before, Rob.' His friend clapped a hand on his knee. 'Well, it's off my chest again and we'll go see about this boat-crew.'

'Wait,' said Knott. 'Just a thought, Will. The Frogs won't have a guard-boat rowing watch on a night like this – or so we trust – and likely her crew's ashore. But there's bound to be a watchman on board, and if we want no alarm given –'

'I've thought of that. And I make no assumptions on the score of guard-boat or crew, Rob. Come on with you.'

Arrangements for a cutting-out expedition were an established routine aboard *Montagu* by now. Sixteen seamen in the cutter, sixteen in the longboat; cutlasses – but no pistols in this case – and knives; three axes, each ground to razor-sharpness, for the cutting of the cables; parties detailed for the hoisting of sail on the brig's two masts. Lieutenant Bissell devoted much time and care to the preparation of a satchel of combustibles. He had made himself something of an expert in such things, and in conference with Mr Ponsonby the gunner had devised a budget of inflammables that would ensure instant and efficient conflagration. Flaherty, boatswain's mate, was entrusted with the satchel. Flint, steel, and tinder would be carried in Bissell's pocket wrapped in oilskin. These preparations were complete well before *Montagu* closed the French coast.

As Mr Kent the master had foretold, the wind had risen slightly during the middle watch and the black waves that shouldered the 74 landward showed white teeth. The moon, in her first quarter, was revealed intermittently in the breaks between fast-flying clouds. At seven bells of the middle watch the masthead lookouts reported land visible on the starboard bow; and Mr Kent having identified this as Isle de Groix, two leagues off the Port Louis headland, the hands swarmed aloft to take in main courses and *Montagu* altered course to creep in due eastward under reefed topsails. An hour later the low black line of the coast had risen against the paler darkness of the sky and she was hove-to. Cutter and longboat were swung out and lowered to the tossing wave-tops, their crews slid down the falls into them.

'Good luck, sir,' said the boatswain, who had charge of the cutter's lowering-party.

Bissell, on the point of following Knott down to the boat, paused. 'Thank you, Massey. How's Diana?'

Diana was a mongrel bitch, the pet of the gunroom.

'Doing fine, sir,' said Massey. 'Any time now, it'll be.'

'See you keep her warm.'

Bissell slid down to the sternsheets, falls and boat-rope were cast off, and the cutter headed away shoreward with the longboat following two lengths astern. Spray blown from the wave-crests flew across the gunwales as they came out from the lee of the ship's hull.

'That satchel in a dry place, Flaherty?'

'Yessir.'

'Very well. Steady pull, lads, and no talking.'

Sitting beside the silent Knott with his arm along the tiller, Lieutenant Bissell allowed what Captain Knight had called the bee in his bonnet to buzz freely.

He had known in advance what Knight's reaction to his suggestion of using a fireship would be, but he had felt bound to make it. Failure to speak one's mind when one felt strongly on a matter was, in William Bissell's view, dishonesty; it was a view that had brought him into conflict with Authority more often than was good for his career in the King's Navy. A captain less tolerant than Knight would have made a disciplinary matter of a second lieutenant's plainly-implied criticism of his tactics, and Bissell was well aware that his credit with his commanding officer, at a low ebb for some time past, had sunk still lower in the past few hours. It did not perturb him, however. He would have been far more perturbed if he had found himself able to acquiesce unprotesting in a plan which, in his opinion, was uneconomical as well as unnecessarily risky. But it was not the tactics of a single small operation so much as the whole of British naval strategy that occupied his mind as the boats sped onward through the windy darkness.

Montagu's second lieutenant held pronounced views on the conduct of the war with France, though he communicated them only to Robert Knott. The blockade was all very well, he reflected as he juggled with the tiller to offset the thrust of following waves; all very well to hold the combined fleets of France and Spain immobilised in port, to harass the French coastal shipping. Doubtless French conquests overseas were prevented thereby but it did nothing to stop their steady enslavement of Europe. While the First Consul could move his fast-growing armies where he liked the Continent was at his mercy. Only four months ago he had concentrated those armies on the Lombard plain and smashed the forces of Austria at Marengo.

What was needed was a series of diversions to separate and scatter Bonaparte's land forces – raids up and down France's enormous coastline, feint landings north and south and west, threats of invasion to thin those armies through the need for coastal defence. New weapons too, for operation from sea to land. Knott's uncle, a crony of the Director at Woolwich Arsenal, had told his nephew how the Admiralty had declined to consider a new design of gun with a rifled barrel, ten times as accurate as the present 32-pounders; and how their Lordships were refusing to countenance the experiments with rockets proposed by the Royal Laboratory. Bissell shifted his damp posterior impatiently on the thwart. Typical of the hidebound old men who ruled the Royal Navy, he told himself. Even fireships – no new invention – weren't being used, though their efficacy had been proved at Toulon in '97. Seven hundred miles of west-facing enemy coastline, onshore winds nearly always blowing, meant that every port and inlet was an obvious target for fireships. And the moral effect on the French, who'd see the successful attacks made while the British ships lay safely out of range of their covering forts and batteries – no one seemed to take account of that. This present petty foray into Port Louis, for instance, could have been made –

'Lights,' said Knott beside him suddenly. 'Fine on the port bow.'

Bissell forgot the shortcomings of his superiors and concentrated all his senses on the present moment. On the black uneven shape of the land that had now risen in a hump above the dark furrows of the waves two bright pinpoints twinkled; the inhabitants of Port Louis would be abed and the lights could mark the positions of the invisible batteries. He brought the cutter's bows a trifle to port, with the lights dead ahead.

'Bow lookout!'

At his sharp order a seaman stood up in the bows, balancing to the pitch and forward surge of the boat. They had still a mile to pull but it was not too soon to watch for a boat rowing guard. If the Frogs' suspicions had been aroused there might be more than one boat, their crews armed with muskets and pistols. He considered the ensuing boat-engagement, the noise of shots and shouts reaching the shore, the enemy defences alerted. And if there were guard-boats it was like enough that the brig had her full crew on board and ready for action.

He dismissed these unprofitable speculations for the less doubtful facts of wind and tide. They must have passed the narrows of the entrance, the broad channel between shoal and rocks which according to Captain Knight gave two miles of sea-room for a vessel beating out to sea. Bissell had not failed to study the chart and he knew that at this state of the tide, an hour past low water, there would be a deal less sea-room than that – with a head wind, barely enough for a fore-and-aft schooner to win safely out. For an unweatherly brig deep-laden there wouldn't be a chance. And the wind was driving full on his back.

Knott nudged an elbow against his ribs. 'There she lies,' he muttered.

A rift in the racing clouds allowed the crescent moon's pale light to give a fleeting glimpse of the brig, anchored bows-on to wind and tide, a dark tall-masted hull against the dim background of the coastal slopes. No lights on her; but it was ten to one she'd have a watchman on board and if the man was doing his duty he would be able to discern the approaching boats. Bissell glanced astern to where the longboat forged onward in his wake. He had ordered

Alexander not to board until he was summoned from the deck of the brig; if there was a watchman he must be silenced first, if possible.

There were no guard-boats. The twin lights climbed higher, the bulk of the brig grew ahead.

'Stand by, bowman,' Bissell said, his voice just loud enough to top the rushing of wind and waves. 'Be ready to fend off, midships. I want no noise.'

He pushed the tiller to port. The longboat astern turned from her course to make for the brig's starboard side while the cutter, rocking and pitching round in a wide circle, came head-to-wind below the French vessel's port rail at the waist. Boat and brig were heaving and tossing and it was not easy to come alongside. There was a thud and a scrape as the boathook felt for hold and found it, a clatter as a boated oar rolled on the thwarts. But Bissell had wasted no time. His sword was belted round his waist and now, hitching the weapon behind his thigh, he stood up, balanced for a second, and sprang for the side.

She was low in the water and he was up and astride the rail at once. The brig's deck was dark and deserted, the big shadowy mainmast rocked slowly against the glimmering sky overhead. He drew his sword and crouched motionless, peering round him in the half-darkness. A movement, on his right front. It was the flapping corner of the hatch-cover, carelessly lashed. He had moved round the corner of the knee-high coaming of the hatch when a dark figure rose from its shelter almost under his nose. Before he could raise his sword he was gripped by the legs and brought down with a crash.

This was how Lieutenant Bissell came to be lying on his back with a knife an inch from his throat.

*

2

His assailant had hurled himself on top of Bissell as he fell. The lieutenant's left hand, upflung in instinctive defence, by good fortune caught the wrist of the hand that held the knife but he knew he could not hold the point from his neck for long. He thrust savagely upward with his knee. There was an agonised groan and the pressure relaxed. Instantly he heaved himself sideways and over, bringing the Frenchman beneath him, seized the man's neck with both hands and slammed his head against the deck planking with all his force. The watchman lay still.

The smell of garlic-scented breath was in his nostrils as he got to his feet and picked up his sword. For five seconds he stood motionless, listening; the watchman had made no outcry and that suggested that he was the only member of the crew on board. There was no sound except the hissing of the wind in shrouds and rigging, and he kicked the watchman's knife into the scuppers and went to the rail.

'All's clear, Mr Knott. I've dealt with the one man on watch. – No talking, there! I'll book the name of the next man that speaks. Come aboard, and quietly.'

He ran across to the starboard side, where the longboat lay tossing two fathoms clear.

'Mr Alexander, you may board now. No noise, if you please.'

The lights on the two batteries, if batteries they were, shone from the black hillside above, almost within earshot. The quays and warehouses of Port Louis were just discernible three cables away across the tossing water – the darkness was beginning to lighten towards dawn. All was dark and silent over there. The surprise had been complete. He had only to cut the cables and make sail – and end up a wreck on La Haie rocks or the shoal, if beating to and fro against the tide and half-a-gale of head wind ever got him that far.

The boat-parties were aboard, bare feet thudding dully on the deck as they trotted to their appointed stations.

'Orders, Mr Bissell?' said Alexander's voice at his elbow.

'Axemen to stand-by at the bitts fore and aft, Mr Alexander. Station the rest of your men at the hatchways and silence any Frenchman who comes on deck.'

'Hands ready to hoist sail?'

'Belay that for the present. And there's a Frenchman lying by the hatch-coaming. See to him, if you please – you'd better gag him and put him under guard.'

Beyond Alexander's departing figure Bissell glimpsed a faint glow of light, instantly vanishing. That was Knott going below with his lantern and the search-party; it was unlikely that Knott would find anyone below decks, and he could trust him to see that none of his men got at wine-store or spirits. He turned and saw a man standing a few feet away.

'Who's that? Flaherty?'

'Aye, sir. Satchel's here, sir, dry as me throat.'

'Very well.'

Bissell's decision was already made. The brig's bowsprit was pointing straight into the wind, straight on the course he must steer to bring her out. Nevertheless he needed to be certain for the sake of his report to the captain. He stepped across to the squat pillar of the binnacle before the brig's wheel and took flint and steel from his pocket, calling Flaherty to stand so that his lean body made a screen between binnacle and shore. The pillar rocked on its rusted deck-bolts and the binnacle-hood was bent and corroded, but even a French coasting brig would have a compass that could be relied on. The first spurt of sparks from his flint showed a fleeting image of the big dial with its thirty-two points, each point helpfully identified. '*O. par N.*' was inscribed over the point cut by the lubber-line on the glass, and that was the precise west by north of Captain Knight's stipulation. Should he get Knott to witness to it? No, by

God! Knight knew this at least of him, that his word was to be trusted.

And here came Knott to report.

'Not a soul below decks,' muttered Knott. 'Only rats. Found the manifest. Ship's stores – spars, canvas, tar, biscuit. Shall I check the holds?'

'Thank you, Mr Knott – no. I'm not taking her out.'

'So she burns, eh?' Knott sounded pleased. 'Should go up quick. Third opening down the alleyway, starboard side, is the cubby-hole where they've stored oil. It's just for'ard of midships.'

'Excellent. What boats does she carry?'

'Only a cockboat. The other boats'll have taken the crew ashore.'

'Get that cockboat into the water, Mr Knott, if you please. Put the Frenchman in it with a pair of sculls and shove him off. Soon as that's done, into the cutter with your party and stand by.'

'The Frog's still as flat as an 'erring, sir,' said a voice from the shadows.

'He'll be a kipper if he's left on board,' growled Knott. 'Bring him to the starboard rail. Huggins, Doyle, Fiori, come with me.'

As Knott departed Alexander came hurrying aft, his white breeches conspicuous in the growing light.

'She mounts four guns,' he said as he came. 'Fourpounders. If we had 'em loaded and run out –'

'I'm going to burn her, Mr Alexander. Who's your strongest axeman?'

'Macarthy,' said Alexander without hesitation.

'Macarthy to the bow cable starboard side,' said Bissell rapidly. 'He's not to cut till I tell him and he'll leave with me in the cutter. Cut both the other cables now, then get your men into the longboat and pull for the ship. Come along, Flaherty.'

He led the way down the dark pit of the hatchway and

groped along the narrow alleyway feeling for the doors on his right. His nose confirmed the cubby-hole opening, which stank of oil, and he knelt inside the doorway.

'Satchel.'

Flaherty laid it beside him and he pulled out the familiar contents. As he arranged them with fingers deft and steady the thud of axe-blows came dully from on deck and the brig, with a lurch and a shudder, swung sideways. Only a single cable held her now. Bissell felt for the package of shavings impregnated with saltpetre, carefully emptied it close to his heap of combustibles, and took flint and steel from his pocket. And he hesitated.

It was only for a second, that hesitation, and yet in it all the seaman's hatred and fear of fire flew through his mind. Storm and gunfire and uncharted reef – these were accepted hazards, the natural ends of many a vessel's life, but fire in a wooden ship was the Devil in visible form. He remembered his horror at seeing the Dutch 64 *Hercules* go up in flames at Camperdown. Even a coasting brig was a ship, a creation of human hands and half human herself, and here he was deliberately invoking her most terrible and implacable foe. The repugnance passed in a flash. This was the weapon he had so often advocated against the enemy. He struck the flint.

The first jet of sparks showed him an instantaneous glimpse of the cubby-hole, a shallow closet with small kegs and gallipots untidily stored: paint and oil. The second strike of the flint ignited the shavings and he got up quickly and stood back. The creeping fire lapped against the pile of combustibles and instantly a tongue of flame leapt up with a hiss to lick the deckhead and fan out across the cubby-hole.

'Glory be!' said Flaherty behind him.

'On deck with you,' Bissell snapped. 'Call the cutter alongside.'

He ran at Flaherty's heels, fingertips touching the sides of the pitch-dark alleyway, and clambered to the deck. The flame had robbed him of night-vision but so far as he could tell the deck was deserted except for Flaherty shouting from the rail; the boat-crews – and the Frenchman in his cockboat – were clear.

'Macarthy! Cut and run, d'ye hear?'

The answering 'aye aye, sir' came to his ears on the piping wind and with it the dull percussion of Macarthy's axe on the cable. Flaherty, astride the rail, reported the cutter alongside and a second later the brig jerked and began to move astern. Macarthy came pelting aft.

'All gone for'ard, sir,' he panted, somewhat unnecessarily.

'Very well. Overside into the cutter.'

Bissell waited a moment before following. His combustibles had included a last-minute supplement of sulphur and he wanted to see if it had increased the efficiency of his handiwork. A little uneasily he remembered the brig's four guns and the powder-store there must be somewhere on board; it wouldn't do to delay too long. The smell of hot tar came to his nostrils, and the acrid scent of charring timber. A crackle, a *whoosh*!, and a spear of flame was thrusting up amidships into a mushrooming cloud of black smoke.

He clambered blindly down into the tossing cutter, landing awkwardly with a knee on the gunwale and saved from falling between boat and ship by Knott's timely grasp. The brig was drifting fast now with her bows swinging off the wind, and they had some ado to pull clear of the swirl and welter under her side, but two minutes of hard work brought the cutter out to seaward with her bows heading into the powerful thrust of wind and tide.

'Quick job you made of her,' Knott said. 'Look at that.'

Astern of them the brig was drifting broadside-on with a cockscomb of flame wavering between her two masts. As they watched, a fresh burst of fire broke out aft and the mainmast shrouds and rigging writhed in snakes of flame. The glare lit the rocks of the shore beyond her and reddened the white of breaking rollers. They saw the fire-wreathed mast bend and fall as she struck, but no sound came to their ears against the fierce wind.

'Finis,' growled Knott.

'She's finished as she'd have done if we'd sent a fireship in,' Bissell said. 'I still think –'

The wrecked brig spouted pale flame and the sound of the explosion, deadened by the wind, told that the fire had found her magazine at last.

'Luck was with us, anyway,' Knott pointed out. 'French ship totally destroyed, and no casualties.'

'We're not back on board yet and an hour's hard pulling to come. Don't forget the batteries.' Bissell raised his voice. 'Backs into it, you men. There's breakfast ahead.'

The oarsmen needed no urging but the cutter could make only slow progress. Opposed by tide and wind, she rammed her bow into the curling waves that charged white-helmed from right ahead, sending drifts of flying spray over the men in her as she pitched from crest to trough and up again. Bissell, whose eyes had recovered from the dazzle of the flames, saw that these waves were no longer black but a dark grey-green, and that the undersides of the ragged clouds that hurried shoreward overhead were paling in the dawn light. Astern the low hump of the land rose dusky grey, with the bright-red glow of the burning brig at its base and a band of lightening sky silhouetting its rounded top. In the west the shadowy rearguard of night fled downward beyond a black horizon, but from a wavecrest he saw *Montagu* under reefed topsails some two miles away ahead, quite clear in the increasing light.

When the cutter rose again he looked for and found the longboat, her long hull half hidden by flying spray as she struggled with the racing seas three cables ahead on the starboard bow. The same brief glance showed him a spout of white water rising some distance beyond the longboat and instantly dispelled sideways by the wind. Knott had seen it too.

'Thirty-two pounder, maybe,' he muttered speculatively.

Hard on his words came the report, muted by the gale. Another followed, and another. They saw nothing of the fall of shot from these.

'A million to one against their hitting us,' said Bissell.

He eased the tiller as the cutter bucked into a wave. He was drenched with spray and chilled to the bone, and wished he had the courage to defy naval convention and give himself a spell at an oar. Coffee hot from the galley was all he asked of the future.

'*Montagu*'s making sail,' said Knott suddenly; he half-rose from the thwart as the cutter dived into a trough. 'Yes – main courses, and she's heading towards us.'

So Knight was going to save his boat-crews some hard labour. Bissell had known captains who, deprived of a coveted prize, would have stood farther out to teach their subordinates a lesson. By Bissell's way of thinking Captain Knight was as avid of prize-money as the rest, but he had to admit that Knight had always shown exceptional care for his people. The dull irregular boom of the guns in the Port Louis batteries had punctuated these thoughts, and they were chased from his mind by the sight of the tall splash of a falling shot a dozen fathoms ahead of the cutter and only a little to starboard of her course. Some French gunner up there knew his business, it seemed.

'And here comes a good-morning for their *bon jour*,' said Knott.

Montagu, now less than a mile away, had turned, presenting her flank to the coast. The crash of her broadside came down the wind and the flame of the guns seemed to darken the grey light. The cutter's oarsmen found wind enough for a ragged cheer.

'Save your breath, there – you've a twenty-minute pull yet,' Bissell snapped; he lowered his voice to a growl. 'Mere waste. Long range, the lee broadside with a half-a-gale heeling her – it's a moral certainty the gunners can't get any elevation at all.'

Knott grinned sideways. 'Maybe the captain feels like – humph – letting off steam. Fine fat brig gone up in smoke and he none the richer for it. I suppose you checked the wind direction?' he added more seriously.

'I did,' Bissell replied stiffly. 'By the brig's compass, Mr Knott. It was west by north precisely.'

'Just a thought,' Knott muttered.

A gout of spray slapped across Bissell's face and when he had wiped his eyes he saw that *Montagu* had clewed-up her courses and come to the wind. The longboat was almost up to her. The boom of the battery guns – three reports in close succession – sounded distant now, but he thought he saw the splash of a shot beyond the ship's swaying hull. It could have been a breaking wave-crest, though.

'A hundred good ones and we're alongside, lads.'

The longboat was alongside already and Alexander and his men were swarming up the ladder. The cutter bucketed on across the diminishing interval of dark-green furrows and by the time she had come within hail of the 74 the longboat was hooked-on to the falls and swinging up from the tossing water.

'Boat your oars! Bows! Fend off, there!'

Bissell stood up in the sternsheets and jumped for the ladder; as senior officer it was his place to come aboard first and Knott's to follow. He stepped over onto the deck and touched his hat to the quarterdeck, where first lieutenant and captain stood looking down from the taffrail. His report to Captain Knight was his first duty, but as he turned to go up the quarterdeck ladder his eye fell on the boatswain and he remembered something.

'Any news of Diana, Massey?'

'Good news, sir,' returned Massey with a beaming smile. 'Seven in the litter. Mother and pups all doing –'

A crescendo whistle, a splintering crash, and Bissell was hurled to the deck. It was a savage blow on the head that laid him there and though he still retained his senses they were dulled and bemused and sight seemed to have forsaken him. He was dimly conscious of running feet, shouted orders, groans and exclamations. Words and phrases penetrated meaninglessly from the hurly-burly. *Tourniquet ... Ted's a goner ... lift! Gently, damn you ... How is he?*

'Stunned, I think, sir,' a voice said loudly close to his ear – Taplin's voice.

He felt himself raised. Vision and feeling came back slowly; a blurred view of the after-deck busy with men clearing wreckage, a stabbing pain in his head. The first lieutenant's large red face appeared above him, grave and frowning.

'Can you stand, Mr Bissell?'

'Yes,' said Bissell. 'I'm – all right.'

Helped by Taplin and a man on his other side – it was Massey – he got to his feet and put a hand to his head, feeling the swelling lump and the warm blood that oozed from it.

'What hit me?' he asked stupidly.

'A piece of the rail,' Taplin said. 'Damned lucky shot for the Frogs, unlucky for us. The ball struck the top of the ladder as Knott was coming aboard, carried away a fathom of rail, pitched through the coaming into the after-hatchway. Killed the two seamen who were coming up behind Knott –' A distant double boom sounded from the French guns and he broke off to roar at the hands on the mainyard overhead. 'Lively aloft there, blast you! – and took off poor Knott's leg,' he finished.

'At the knee, sir, and clean as a whistle,' said Massey; he caught sight of Bissell's face and added quickly: 'He'll be all right, sir – surgeon's got him in hand this minute.'

'Best get a plaster on that head wound before you make your report,' said Taplin. 'You did well, Mr Bissell. She made a nice bonfire –'

Bissell ceased to hear him. Rob Knott, a legless cripple – if the surgeon saved him. His service career cut short. A pensioner with a crutch, never to go to sea again. Fierce anger rose in him. *Montagu* heeled as the wind filled her sails and the boatswain caught his arm to steady him. He threw off the man's grasp roughly.

'A nice bonfire!' His voice rang loud and harsh. 'God damn you, what was the cost? Two lives and a man's leg gone – wasted! If my advice had been taken –'

'Boatswain!' Taplin shouted him down swiftly. 'You'll see Mr Bissell to his cabin, if you please. See that he has that wound seen to.'

He turned away. Bissell, his fury ebbing, allowed Massey to steer him across the deck with a hand on his elbow, past the carpenter's party trotting up to repair the shattered rail. Two men were scrubbing with mops at a dark stain beside the heap of splintered wood. A big seaman, his face expressive of tragedy, ran to the boatswain as they reached the top of the companionway and jerked two sentences at him in an undertone beyond Bissell's hearing.

'Is it – Mr Knott?' he demanded, anxiety stabbing him.

'No, sir. It's Diana, dead as mutton.' Massey sounded more moved than he had been by the deaths of his shipmates. 'God's curse on the French bastards! Beg your pardon, sir – but we had her and the pups in the cubby below the after-hatch and the spent ball landed on 'em. – Steady down the ladder, sir. – All the pups killed 'cept one. Here we are, sir. Better sit down.'

Bissell sat on his sea-chest in the cabin. His anger smouldered still but the death of a mongrel bitch added little fuel to it.

'I'll be wanted on deck, sir,' said Massey. 'I'll send a hand with water and a plaster, if you can manage.'

'I can manage.'

'Pore little bastard!' the boatswain muttered as he left the cabin.

Bissell started; then he remembered the motherless pup.

But he couldn't smile, for his thoughts were of Robert Knott and the dark future that lay ahead of his friend. After a moment, and with an effort, he turned his mind to more immediate matters. He had his report to make.

3

John Knight, post-captain and virtual arbiter of life and death for the 570 men who served in *Montagu*, had commanded his present ship for five years. He had a wife and six children to keep and a family debt to pay off, and his pay was inadequate to the financial burden unless supplemented with prize-money. When *Montagu* was ordered away from the main fleet off Brest for an independent cruise it had come as a godsend, and in making the most of his chances he had perhaps become a trifle over-eager to get his hands on enemy vessels and cargoes that would show a substantial figure when they came to be valued by the Prize Court. But Captain Knight was not avaricious by nature, nor was he (despite Lieutenant Bissell's strictures) exceptionally callous in the expenditure of the lives and limbs of his ship's company. Like many another captain in King George's Royal Navy, he was both sensitive and humane; but in his forty years of service he had learned that a post-captain must conceal any such qualities beneath an unbending mask of stern authority, and the mask had fitted itself so snugly that he found it difficult to lift it. Sitting at the table in the big cabin with his second lieutenant standing stiffly before him, he was considering how he should deal with this awkward subordinate.

Lieutenant Bissell's beauty, never outstanding, was not improved by the untidy hump of plaster that decorated his reddish-brown hair, which he wore without powder or queue in a cluster of lank curls. His angular face was paler than usual and his unmusical voice was as devoid of expression as his face as he made his report.

'The watchman having been silenced, the crews of both boats boarded without encountering any opposition. Mr Knott –' he made an almost imperceptible pause on the name – 'reported her cargo to be ship's stores. There was no one else on board, and I sent the watchman off in the cockboat before setting fire to her and cutting the cables.'

'Very well. A commendable operation, Mr Bissell.' Captain Knight lowered his gaze to the papers on the table in front of him; he was well aware that Robert Knott was Bissell's closest friend on board. 'A great pity that it should end as it did. I need hardly say how much I regret the serious injury to Mr Knott.'

Bissell's jaw muscles tightened but he said nothing.

'*Montagu* is ordered to Portsmouth for a refit at the end of this cruise,' Knight continued. 'I shall personally ensure that Mr Knott has the best treatment that can be procured.' He looked up suddenly, his expression hardening. 'But with you, Mr Bissell, I have a bone to pick.'

The lieutenant was jolted from his rigidity. 'The wind was precisely west by north, sir. I checked it –'

'I'm not referring to that, Mr Bissell!' Knight snapped irritably. 'I don't question your decision. I'm referring to your conduct aboard this ship. You recall, I trust, the language you saw fit to use to the first lieutenant, your senior officer?'

'Yes, sir,' Bissell said stonily.

'I was on the quarterdeck and heard your words myself. Under the Articles of War, Mr Bissell, you could be brought before a Court Martial and charged with insubordinate conduct. I make allowance for you on the score of the blow on the head you had just received, but it's by no means the first time I've made such allowance.' The captain's sharp gaze went past him to the door in the bulkhead, on the other side of which the marine sentry stood. 'Two paces nearer my table, if you please.'

Bissell obeyed stiffly. The captain took up a paper from the table but his eyes fixed themselves steadily on the lieutenant's face.

'You'll listen to what I have to say because I'm your captain,' he said in a lowered tone. 'I shall say it because I'm old enough to be your father, though God knows you're no youngster. You're riding for a fall, Mr Bissell, whether you know it or not. No captain of a King's ship is going to tolerate criticism, spoken or implied, from a junior lieutenant, nor will he suffer unmoved an officer who regards as outmoded and inefficient the established usages of the Royal Navy. That, I fancy, is how you regard them, Mr Bissell.'

It was half a question; but Bissell, his features impassive, made no reply.

'You've left the wardroom in no doubt as to your opinions, at least,' Knight said drily. 'You should know by now that a naval officer holding such opinions should be most careful to keep them to himself. If he does not – ' He broke off with a shrug and frowned at the paper he was holding. 'I have your record here. You entered the Navy in '81. Served in *Inflexible*, *Culloden*, *Fortune* – ' he ran his finger down the list – 'and six others. You were in the action off Cuddalore with the East Indies squadron and in *Gibraltar*, first-rate, at the Fréjus battle. Captain Duckworth of *Orion* certifies your "spirited exertions" in the sea-fight on the Glorious First of June.' He looked up. 'Your exertions at Camperdown were also spirited, Mr Bissell. as I would have been prepared to certify. Equally spirited, however, as I am given to understand, were your strictures on my handling of *Montagu* during the battle.'

Bissell was silent. Others beside him – and greatly senior to him – had criticised *Montagu*'s behaviour in that bloodiest of all sea-fights but he knew it was reprehensible for one of her own officers to do so.

'You've served with me nearly four years,' Knight

continued, 'and I don't ask for a better sea-officer or one who knows more of a seaman's duty. What you haven't learned is the necessity of compromise – a universal necessity, Mr Bissell, if a man is to prosper in this world. Outspoken criticism is very well, but not when its targets are the men who could break you.' He changed his tone abruptly. 'You have a brother in the Navy, I believe – Captain Austin Bissell, *Blenheim* 74.'

'Yes, sir.'

'A post-captain. Your younger brother, I think?'

'Yes.' Bissell said woodenly.

'It would seem that Captain Bissell learned the lesson you failed to master.' The captain straightened himself in his chair and resumed his usual curt manner. 'I've one last thing to say to you, Mr Bissell. You may take it that it would have been said earlier if competent officers were easy to come by. On arrival at Portsmouth there will be no objection to your applying for transfer to another ship. That is all.'

The lieutenant receved this dismissal without visible emotion. Having no hat to touch, he bowed stiffly from the hips and walked out of the cabin onto the windy after-deck where the carpenter and his party were busy at the smashed rail. There was the inevitable pang of sorrow at the prospect of leaving *Montagu*, his home for three years and more, but it was short-lived; Knott would have to leave her too. Knott and Diana the mongrel bitch, he reflected, had been the only creatures in *Montagu* that had engaged his affection, and a French cannon-ball had robbed the ship of both of them. His anger had evaporated, and he felt no resentment at Knight's blunt instruction to find himself another berth – a lesser chastisement, he knew, than he might have expected. His report having been duly made, his chief anxiety was for the state of Robert Knott, below in the sick-bay.

The ship was beating close-hauled across a tossing grey sea under a grey sky where there was no hint of the imminent sunrise. He noted as he crossed the deck the *Marie Payot* and the two other prizes in company to leeward. There was no land in sight from the deck; *Montagu* had the wind on her starboard bow, heading south of west to clear the Isles de Glenan and the Penmarch headland. Down the ladders and alleyways to the sick-bay – and here was Pudney the surgeon coming out of the sick-bay door.

'You can't see him,' Pudney said firmly, closing the door behing him. 'I've used laudanum and he'll not come out of it for some while yet.'

'Is he – will he live?'

Pudney grunted. 'There's always the chance of gangrene. But it's clean enough and the odds are on recovery. I'd say it'll heal as sound as a bell, giving him a stump a foot long from the crotch.'

Bissell felt slightly sick as he climbed back on deck. His head was throbbing painfully and he gave a short reply to the boatswain who waylaid him with inquiries after Mr Knott as he emerged from the companion.

'Yessir,' said Massey, detaining him, 'but – beg your pardon, sir – you was fond of Diana, and maybe you'd give the gunroom a word of advice consarning *this*.'

He spread a capacious palm, displaying what the lieutenant at first took to be a perique of ship's tobacco. Then it moved and whimpered feebly, a tiny creature glistening-sleek and blind.

'There's no ma to feed it,' pursued Massey, eyeing the puppy doubtfully. 'Mr Ponsonby, he reckons 'twould be a kindness to put it overside, out of its misery.'

'Nonsense!' snapped Bissell. 'Has Martha stopped giving?' Martha was the ship's nanny-goat. 'Get some goat's milk – Flaherty's your man for udder-squeezing – and dilute it half-and-half with warm water.'

'It can't lap, sir.'

'Well, God damn it all!' Bissell put a hand to his splitting head. 'Get a hollow quill – Here!' he interrupted himself suddenly. 'Give him to me. Send Flaherty to my cabin with that warm milk-and-water and a quill.'

'Aye aye, sir. But the –'

'And pass the word for the wardroom steward. He's to bring me some hot coffee, piping hot.' The puppy warm in his hand emitted a tiny wail. 'I'll look after this little fellow.'

'Yessir. But – it's a bitch, sir,' said the boatswain, departing.

Bissell, making for his cabin, took a glance at the helpless small animal he held against his coat. It was brown, with a star of white hair in the centre of its forehead. So you're a bitch, my lady, he said in his mind; you shall be Stella Maris, star of the sea. The puppy whimpered feebly and seemed to nuzzle against his side. He hadn't thought himself in need of comfort, but now, for some reason, he felt comforted.

II

Kathy

1

The doorkeeper of the Stores Building at Woolwich Arsenal opened his door for a look at the May morning outside. There was not much to see; a rectangle of high stone wall enclosing a grassed plot, an arched doorway in the wall, a sliver of sunlit green showing above it where Woolwich Common rose against a cloudless blue sky. From the gun-factory on the other side of the Arsenal came the ceaseless *thud-thud-thud* of steam-driven machinery, but over it sounded the singing of larks on the Common. The doorkeeper, who was a country-bred man, cocked his ear with a smile. Then he heard the slap of hand on musket-butt as the sentry outside the wall-door saluted, and recognised the man who came through the doorway with a small dog frisking at his heels, a tall angular man in blue coat with spotless white breeches and stockings. The tall man was a frequent visitor at the Arsenal, though this was the first time the doorkeeper had seen him wearing naval-officer rig. The visitor halted halfway along the paved walk.

'Still!' he said sharply.

The small dog, who had been trotting in front of her master, halted instantly, with one paw raised and her head turned to watch him. He stooped, clipped a thin leather lead to her collar, and came on.

'Mornin', Mr Bissell,' said the doorkeeper; he jerked his

head towards the interior of the building. ''E's 'ard at it this mornin' but you can 'ave a word. And 'ow's Stella, eh?' he added, bending to pat the dog.

Mixed breeding showed plainly in her and yet she was not unhandsome; tawny coat close and curling, small sharp ears and stumpy tail, short muzzle with a white star precisely in the centre of the forehead, black nose perpetually a-quiver and very bright eyes. The eyes were just now upturned questioningly to Bissell, who responded with a nod. Stella gave a perfunctory lick to the caressing hand and sat down to await events.

'Hextra busy we are, all of a sudden,' said the doorkeeper. 'D'ye know if it means anything, sir?'

Bissell hesitated for a second. 'I'm told Lord Whitworth's back from Paris. We'll hear in due course whether or not he's patched up the quarrel with Boney.'

'If it comes,' said the doorkeeper, 'it'll make a nice change arter fourteen months o' peace.'

Bissell and Stella went along the tiled passage and in through the open door of a small room on the left made smaller still by the ledgers, filing boxes, and stacks of papers that occupied the shelves on every wall. In the middle was a desk with a massive ledger open upon it, and in front of the desk, perched on a high stool, was Robert Knott. A pair of crutches were suspended from a neatly-spliced becket on a hook at the side of the desk, and the stool had a padded flange on its port side (Knott's own device) for the support of the stump of his left thigh.

'Heard you come aboard, Will,' Knott said as they shook hands briefly. 'What's the news from up-river?'

He leaned down to pat Stella, who was sniffing, as she always did, at his tidily breeched stump.

'I was at the Admiralty yesterday,' said Bissell. 'The whole place is buzzing with rumours. They say Cornwallis has been ordered to hoist his flag at Torbay and prepare for the blockade of Brest. And –'

'God save us, what's this?' Knott pointed to his friend's breeches. 'Last week and all the others it was buckskins and a brown cutaway.'

Bissell grinned a trifle sheepishly. 'Call it vanity if you like. Last week I was unemployed, a half-pay idler. Now I feel like a sea-officer again. I'm appointed to a ship, Rob.'

Knott's square face, paler than it had been two years ago, showed his pleasure in a beaming smile. 'Best news I've heard for a long time,' he declared. 'What ship?'

'*Donegal,* Captain Malcolm. I'm to join three days from now. I'll have my hands full and small time for visiting here, Rob – I'm to be first lieutenant.'

'First of an eighty-gun ship!' Knott could not keep the surprise out of his tone.

'I know. Doesn't sort with my presumed credit at Admiralty, does it?'

'Knight gave you a thundering good certificate. He pulled a string or two to get me into this job, bless him. Maybe he's pulled a string in your behalf. – Just a thought,' Knott added quickly as his friend frowned.

'I fancy it was luck,' Bissell said. 'They needed an experienced officer and I chanced to be handy. I'm experienced enough, God knows – thirty-four years old and twenty-two of 'em in the Navy. Half the line-of-battle ships were laid up at the beginning of the Peace and now they've got to be commissioned in a mad hurry. That's what they're doing. And with Cornwallis warned for the blockade –'

'It's war, then.'

'War's a moral certainty, in my view.'

'And Stella sails with you in *Donegal*?'

The dog, who had been sitting immobile at Bissell's feet, looked up sharply at her name.

'That's of course,' Bissell said. 'She's wholly ship-trained, as you know. She won't be the first dog to go to sea in a King's ship, and if Captain Malcolm don't like it he can lump it.'

Knott shifted himself uneasily on his stool. 'Will – take a friend's advice and keep a curb on your tongue in *Donegal*. Remember how you and I used to talk of how we'd manage our ships when we were made post? I'm beyond it now, but I look to see you with a pair of epaulettes before Boney's done for, and if I get my wish it'll be nigh as good as wearing 'em myself.'

It was a long speech for Robert Knott, and the scowl with which Bissell had heard its beginning gave place at the end to one of his rare smiles.

'I'll bear that in mind, Rob,' he said. 'All the same, I'll not stand quietly by while the Navy turns its back on modern weapons and captains fight their ships as Drake and Blake fought theirs.'

'Speaking of that,' said Knott, 'there's a man in the Laboratory here – son of the Comptroller – experimenting with rockets. Congreve's his name.'

'Rockets!' Bissell's harsh voice held a note that made Stella prick up her ears. 'Now there's an idea. The propellent for your shot, your twelve-pounder ball, is instantaneous, finished after its single explosion. A rocket's propellent would be continuous, capable of –'

He stopped as a weedy young man burst into the room carrying a sheaf of papers.

'Your pardon,' said the young man with a glance at the visitor, 'but these is urgent, Mr Knott. Mr Cargill says please to make the entries with all speed – there's more to come.'

He dashed out again. Knott looked at Bissell and nodded.

'Ship requisitions,' he said. 'Powder, balls, gun-carriages, port-fires, the whole caboodle. Trade's looking up.'

'And it's time for me to up anchor.' Bissell gripped his friend's hand. 'We may not meet again for a month or two, so – farewell, shipmate.'

'You'll be taking a wherry back to London Bridge?'

'Aye, but the tide's not making yet. Stella and I will go up on the Common for a walk.' On the last word the dog sprang to her feet and stood expectant. 'It's a fine fresh morning,' Bissell went on, 'and I only wish you could –'

He checked himself quickly and bit his lip. Knott smiled at him.

'I'll come with you one of these days,' he said cheerfully. 'I can make three knots on crutches, with the wind astern. But not today, Will. I wish you a prosperous cruise and a happy return.'

Bissell and Stella went out, past the doorkeeper and the sentry and up a broad rutted track onto the grassy slope of Woolwich Common. There had been overnight rain, and water lay in the clay of the ruts and in larger puddles that reflected the blue sky. He stopped below the brow of the ascent and freed the dog from her lead.

'Independent cruise, miss,' he said; and with a sweep of his arm, 'Away with you!'

Stella needed no second bidding. Above all things she loved great open spaces like the Common and the freedom to race away into the distance. Bissell watched her vanish over the green rim just above him with no qualms about her eventual return to his side; in a crowd or in a desert Stella's keen sight and unerring nose would locate her master. The pride and affection he felt for her might have been the feelings of a fond parent for his first-born, he told himself (with an inward smile at his own absurdity) as he climbed the slope of the Common. Or perhaps his fondness for a mongrel bitch resulted in part from his detachment from the females of his own species. William Bissell's early years in the Navy had given him such experience of women as might be expected: in the brothels of British and foreign ports and – later – in the less inelegant *bagnios* of the cities. At 28 he had resolved that these indulgences were disgusting, and with characteristic aversion to half-measures had forsworn the company of women. He considered himself to have outgrown it.

On the crest of the slope he halted for breath. To his right a green hillside rose to the invisible top of Shooter's Hill and down on the left was the silver Thames dotted with moving craft and flanked on the Essex shore by fields and villages. Turning, he looked westward to the distant spires and domes of London under the pall of dingy smoke that always hung over them. A further rise of ground lay ahead, and when he had topped this he was on the rim of the undulating plateau where the military sometimes exercised, with the unfenced carriage-road that ran across it close on his left hand. There were several open carriages halted on the road with people sitting in them. The distant *rat-a-tat-tat* of a drum somewhere in front mingled with the dull thumping of machinery in the Arsenal behind him, but his view forward was limited by a low bank that crossed the plateau. The drum and the carriages, however, suggested that some sort of military spectacle was toward, manoeuvres or a review; and the high notes of a bugle, followed by hoarse shouting, confirmed this idea. There was no Stella to be seen on the hundred yards of grass between him and the carriages, and Bissell crossed the bank to halt between two of the lagoons of bald clay that dotted the worn ground beyond.

Advancing towards him a cable-length away was a long line of red, grenadiers in their scarlet coats and tall mitre-hats, their long white gaiters rippling in unison as they marched with their muskets held upright against their shoulders. A drum tapped the step, sergeants dodged on the flanks yelling when the line lost a particle of its perfect dressing. At the end of the line near the road an officer with a good deal of gold braid dangling about him rode on a black horse whose nervous skips and hops he seemed to have difficulty in controlling. There was still no sign of Stella, so Bissell put two fingers in his mouth and loosed a piercing whistle.

For two seconds this signal produced no visible effect. Then from behind the advancing line came a shrill angry bark. The white gaiters in the centre of the line could be seen to falter and a slight but undeniable gap appeared. Through it burst a small brown shape to come hurtling across the grass to her master, while behind her the gap in the line became a deepening sag and the sergeants screamed ineffective curses. Bissell had bent to pat Stella, who was plainly intimating that she had come as quickly as she could, when the sound of approaching hoofbeats brought him erect. The grenadier officer reined-in his mount violently close to the pair. He was a fattish young man with curled black whiskers and jowls as red as his coat. The hands that wrenched at the reins held also a silver-topped cane.

'God damn you, sir!' he gobbled breathlessly. 'Why the devil, sir – can't you control your God-damned dog, sir?'

As he spoke he wagged his cane in furious admonition. Ears and eyes told Stella that her master was being threatened and she sprang to his defence, leaping with bared teeth at the grenadier's stirrup. With an oath he swung his cane aloft and leaned over to aim a savage cut at the dog.

The next five seconds were a whirl of violent action. Bissell leapt forward, caught the cane as it descended, wrenched it from the grenadier's hand. The horse reared and plunged with its rider clinging frantically to the pommel, trampling in the muddy pool and sending wet clay flying in all directions.

Finding the animal's rump very conveniently positioned, Bissell smote it with the cane. The black horse squealed and bolted, the grenadier (who had lost his stirrups) embracing its neck with both arms. Meanwhile the sergeants had about-turned their long red line and were trying to dress it. Their efforts were scarcely begun when the black horse bore down from the rear and scattered the centre in a swirl of sprinting white gaiters, thereafter vanishing beyond a crowd of redcoats struggling to re-form line.

'Pipe down, miss!' Bissell told the dog. 'We don't brag after the victory,' he added with a grin.

Stella's paean of triumphant barking ceased instantly, though her tail continued to wag and her eyes to sparkle in a smile as evident as her master's. Bissell stood with his hands on his hips looking after the retreating soldiery. He thought it unlikely that the officer would return even if he managed to get his mount under control, but if he came back to demand satisfaction he should have it. A certain wetness on his face appraised him that wet clay had been spattered across it. In drawing his handkerchief from his pocket he glanced down – and instantly the smile was replaced by an expression of utter dismay. White breeches and stockings, new blue coat and buckled shoes, were all so bespattered with red clay that there was as much red about him as white or blue.

William Bissell wasn't ordinarily fussy about his appearance but this was too much. He, first lieutenant of an 80-gun ship, to stalk through the streets like a raree-show, the Tricolor'd Man – he couldn't face anyone like this. For the moment the efficient sea-officer was at a loss, standing with arms akimbo and staring aghast at his mud-plastered clothes while Stella, ears drooping and tail between legs, gazed up at him in evident concern.

'No, Kathy – come back, I command you!'

The strident female voice made Bissell start and swing round apprehensively. He saw now that a two-horse open carriage stood on a bend of the road not two hundred yards from him. There was a coachman on the box and two people in the carriage, and running towards him from it was a girl in a flowered muslin gown. Her bonnet had fallen back, restrained by its ribbons knotted at her neck, and shining dark-brown ringlets tossed in the May sunshine. She began to speak while she was still several paces away.

'I saw it all – he was going to strike your little dog, the brute!' she said breathlessly. 'I quite thought the black horse would trample on him,' she added, coming to a halt in front of him. 'He's not hurt, is he?'

Large dark-blue eyes looked anxiously up at him. She was small and slim, with delicate features and perfect complexion just now beautifully flushed with exertion. She was – he perceived it instantly – by far the prettiest girl he had ever seen.

'He's a she,' he said foolishly, staring at her.

'Oh. She's a darling, then.'

She bent to pat the dog, who backed away with a low growl and a jealous upward glance; Stella was a very intelligent animal.

'But I came because of the splash,' the girl went on quickly. 'Forgive me, sir, but it's made a monstrous terrible mess of you. – And alack! I've forgot my manners.'

She curtseyed, hastily but with a grace that Bissell found bewitching. He collected his scattered wits to respond in form, and the off-sweep of cocked hat that accompanied his awkward bow dislodged a lump of clay that flew with a plop into the puddle. The girl laughed and was instantly serious again.

'Indeed, it's no jesting matter,' she said. 'You must come into our carriage – Mr Tierney's carriage, I mean. It won't at all do for an officer of the Royal Navy to make a public appearance in such a state – you *are* a naval officer, aren't you?' she finished with a touch of anxiety.

'I – yes, ma'am.' Bissell had a ridiculous sensation of drowning in the depths of dark-blue eyes; he pulled himself together. 'I'm most grateful, but in this condition I wouldn't be welcome in anyone's carriage. I –'

'You will in Mr Tierney's, I promise. He's very nice and a member of Parliament too – an Irish member. Aunt Honoria will scold me for a forward minx, but never mind that.' She settled the bonnet on her head. 'Come, sir, I beg. And the little dog – what is her name?'

'Stella,' said Bissell absently.

He was perceiving what he should have seen before: that he could return to Knott's office at the Arsenal and make shift to effect some sort of toilet there. But then he would probably never see this lovely creature again.

'My own name is William Bissell, ma'am,' he said with sudden decision, 'and I'm your obedient servant. It would be churlish to decline your exceeding kindness –'

'It would indeed,' she interrupted briskly, 'so let's make haste, Mr Bissell. I'm Katharine Corbett Barnes and I refuse to curtsey again amid all this mud. Pray follow me to the carriage, sir.'

She led the way across the turf with the folds of her dress gathered in one hand, displaying a neat ankle and a small foot. Everything about her was small and delicate, thought Bissell as he followed a pace behind with Stella trotting unenthusiastically at his heels.

'Aunt Honoria, Mr Tierney – this is Mr Bissell,' said Miss Barnes, and he came out of a beatific daydream with a start to make his bow.

Mr Tierney, a stout gentleman with an eye both shrewd and merry, raised his hat. Aunt Honoria fixed the newcomer with an aggressive eye; her large mottled face glowered at him from beneath an overwhelming bonnet.

'There are Bissells in Cheshire,' she announced in a voice like the rasp of a file.

'My father was Rector of Tattenhall in Cheshire, ma'am,' said Bissell. 'He died last year. But by your leave, I'm ashamed to present myself in this condition. I fear I'm in no –'

'Ta,ta,ta,ta,' Mr Tierney broke in heartily. 'read your Pope, sir – honour and shame from no condition rise. Get in, Kathy. Get in, sir. Our first requirement is to conceal your – ha – unmentionables from the public gaze. You'd best sit beside me,' he added, prudently tucking under him the skirts of his green coat.

Kathy sprang in to sit beside her aunt. Bissell seated himself gingerly where he had been bidden with Stella (who knew her place in boat or coach) squeezed in behind his legs.

He had no idea whither he was bound and he didn't much care; Kathy was sitting opposite him, her dark-blue eyes smiling reassurance at him and her muslin-covered knees not six inches from his muddied ones. Mr Tierney, whose back was to the horses, reached up and rapped his knuckles twice against the coachman's spine. The carriage moved on.

2

Perhaps Mr Tierney considered that as a member of Parliament and an Irishman he was expected to be both voluble and amusing. At any rate, he took upon himself the burden of conversation and quickly placed a somewhat unorthodox introduction on a more regular footing. He elicited from Bissell his rank and ship and where he was lodging in London, managed tactfully to convey that Aunt Honoria was the Honourable Miss Simpson, and asserted that he had never seen anything more comical than 'little Stella routing a half-company of the Twenty-third Foot.'

Despite his preoccupation with looking at Kathy while appearing to admire the landscape behind her, Bissell perceived that the genial MP was taking pains to put him at ease, and was grateful. While the carriage jolted slowly down the hill and turned left along a country lane, he learned from Mr Tierney's fluent discourse (Kathy and her aunt assisting when allowed) what his rescuers proposed to do with him.

The ladies, it appeared, were staying with Miss Simpson's relative Sir Alexander Legge at his house near Hither Green, four miles ahead of the carriage. Mr Tierney had called to take them for a drive and now intended to return them to their host before driving the further seven miles to London Bridge, whence he would proceed to Westminster for the afternoon sitting of the House.

'And I can set you down at the very door of your lodging, sir,' he told Bissell, 'before any citizen of London has a chance to see a naval officer other than immaculate.'

'It's most kind of you to take so much trouble.'

'No trouble in all the world, me boy. – You know where Cloak Lane is, Clancy, do you not?' added Mr Tierney, raising his voice above the *clop-clop* of hooves.

'Is it Cloak Lane, yer honour? Sure, 'tis the flit of a wren's wing off Cannon Street,' replied the coachman without turning.

'I do very well without the brogue meself,' Mr Tierney said complacently. 'Should any mistrustful Englishman doubt I'm from Ireland I can produce Clancy to prove my *bona fides*.'

He paused to chuckle over this whimsy. Miss Simpson had been sitting with her gloved hands resting on a stout ivory-topped stick and her tall bonnet nodding to the motion of the carriage. Twice Mr Tierney's verbosity had thwarted her attempt to address Bissell and now she succeeded, favouring him with a basilisk stare as she spoke.

'The Fittons of Gawsworth are one of the oldest families in the country,' she pronounced in rasping tones. 'Gawsworth, I believe is in Cheshire. You are acquainted with the Fitton family, Mr Bissell, no doubt.'

'I'm related, ma'am,' Bissell replied, concealing inward satisfaction; the need to conciliate Kathy's aunt was apparent. 'My mother – dead these many years – was a Fitton.'

Miss Simpson nodded and would have spoken further but that her niece forestalled her, leaning forward eagerly.

'*Donegal*, I know, is a ship of the line, sir,' she said. 'But – did you ever serve in frigates?'

'I was midshipman in *Winchelsea*, Miss Barnes, but since then –'

'Did you ever meet Lord Cochrane, Captain Lord Cochrane?'

Bissell had heard of Cochrane. In the year before the Peace there had been a *Gazette* with a quite incredible account of his exploits; the consensus of wardroom opinion was that he was one of your show-away lordlings, determined to be dashing.

'I've not met him,' he said, 'but I recall hearing of an action he was engaged in. He commanded *Speedy*, did he not?'

'Indeed Lord Cochrane commanded *Speedy*!' The blue eyes flashed indignantly. '*Speedy* carried eighty-eight men and mounted fourteen four-pounders, Mr Bissell. She attacked a Spanish frigate, *El Gamo*, of thirty-two guns and a crew of three hundred and nineteen. Lore Cochrane boarded and took her – there never was such a famous action!'

'Hear her!' laughed Mr Tierney. 'She has the jargon as pat as an admiral, and the numbers too. I'll wager 'tis all copied down in your commonplace-book, Miss Katharine. That's a mighty volume, Mr Bissell, bound in blue leather and sacred to the doings of a certain young nobleman.'

'At least that was no commonplace sea-fight, Uncle Tierney,' the girl retorted. 'And it happened two years ago almost to the day.'

The blush which Tierney's remarks had brought to Kathy's face made her, in Bissell's opinion, more lovely than ever but it increased his growing uneasiness.

'Lord Cochrane is a friend?' he ventured.

The girl's colour deepened still more. 'A – an acquaintance, sir. We haven't met for some little while –'

'Five years ago and you were a child of thirteen,' interrupted Miss Simpson firmly.

'Yes, aunt. But we haven't had any news of Tom Cochrane since the Peace, and I thought that Mr Bissell, being a sea officer, might –'

'That will do, miss. You are too forward, as I've told you often enough. We have known this gentleman an hour at most –'

Here the impending lecture was cut short by a lusty shout of 'Gate, there!' from the coachman. They had passed through a straggling village of thatched cottages and now had halted at an imposing gateway with a lodge to one side of it. A woman ran out of the lodge to open the gates and curtseyed as the carriage rolled through. Turning to look ahead, Bissell saw a quarter of a mile of gravelled driveway curling through parkland towards a mansion, palpably new, with pillared portico and balustrade.

'The Hall.' Mr Tierney took a watch from his fob, glanced at it, and put it back. 'Yes,' he added, catching Bissell's eye. 'You'd best not get out, Mr Bissell – you won't be detained for long.'

Bissell remembered his mud-splashed hat and took it off. Kathy smiled at him and then frowned.

'You've a mud-spot, sir – just beside your left eye,' she said. 'Perhaps I can remove it.'

To her aunt's manifest disapproval she leaned forward with a handkerchief in her outstretched hand. Bissell's own handkerchief was in his pocket but he had his wits about him.

'Allow me, Miss Katherine,' he said, gently taking the lace-edged scrap from her. 'Here?'

She nodded, white teeth pressing into red lower lip as she watched him dislodge the mud and glance at the soiled handkerchief.

'You must permit me to have this laundered, ma'am,' he said, and dropped it into his side-pocket. 'I hope I may have the pleasure of returning it to you in person – shall we say one afternoon of next week?'

How he was to get himself away from the mass of work that awaited him on board *Donegal* he didn't know, but he had to see Kathy Barnes again before the ship sailed. It was Miss Simpson who answered his question.

'We shall not be at the Hall next week, sir,' she told him stiffly. 'We leave the day after tomorrow. – Katharine, your bonnet is quite askew. Set it to rights, miss, before Sir Alexander sees you.'

The carriage crunched to a standstill on the gravel at the foot of a broad flight of steps. Mr Tierney got out and stood to assist the older lady, who inclined her bonnet briefly at Bissell before climbing heavily down. Kathy paused to hold out her hand, and Bissell, reaching to take it with the full intention of kissing it, was disconcerted when she merely administered a pat to the recumbent Stella. He had his consolation a moment later, however.

'We remove to Aunt's town house,' she said in a low voice. 'It's Number Four Bryanstone Square – you are welcome to call. Especially,' she added quickly, 'if you bring news of Captain Lord Cochrane. Goodbye, sir.'

She was gone, running up the portico steps to overtake the others. A tall man in a plum-coloured coat, presumably Sir Alexander Legge, had come down the top steps to assist Mr Tierney with Aunt Honoria, who was making heavy weather of the ascent. All four disappeared into the house.

Damn Captain Lord Cochrane! But at least, thought Bissell, fingering the little handkerchief in his pocket, he would see Kathy again – and with that thought came sudden realisation of his own plunge into folly. A girl of eighteen! He was nearly twice her age. Scarcely more than an hour ago he'd been walking on Woolwich Common with no prevision of the fate in store; if any man had told him that he, William Bissell, was to fall head-over-ears in love in a few minutes' time he'd have dismissed the fellow as an escaped Bedlamite. Yet the unbelievable thing had happened. It was like a dream; and feeling the need to assure himself of reality he reached down to stroke Stella, who licked his hand.

Mr Tierney came hurrying down the steps, got into the carriage, and bade Clancy drive on.

'Now to the needy villain's general home,' he said, settling himself opposite Bissell as the carriage trundled away from the Hall. 'Sam Johnson called London that and with justice. As temporary residents – I from Ireland and you from Cheshire – we may not dissent, sir.' His small grey eyes twinkled at his companion. 'Honoria Simpson fairly lapped up your Fitton blood, if you'll pardon the quip.'

'Your niece is in her care, sir, I take it?'

'Kathy's not my niece. "Uncle" is, so to speak, a relative term.' Mr Tierney chuckled at his own wit and then became serious. 'I was her father's friend, sir. When Corbett Barnes lost every penny on the Stock Exchange and died a month afterwards he left his motherless daughter as destitute as himself. His wife's sister took charge of Kathy, which shows there's a heart somewhere below that monstrous bonnet.' He wagged his head, frowning. 'Or mayhap she needs a nurse for her ailments. Honoria Simpson, Mr Bissell, has two consuming interests. One, as you'll have gathered, is the county families of this island. The other is doctors and quacksalvers.'

'Miss Simpson is lame, I noticed,' said Bissell politely, thinking of Kathy's slim figure running up the steps.

'Her gout's genuine enough, sure. 'Tis the thousand imaginary illnesses she has that occupy her mind. Women have these obsessions, sir.'

'Miss Katharine's being – Captain Lord Cochrane?' Bissell suggested boldly.

Mr Tierney glanced at him sharply. 'Ha! Are ye there? That's another female weakness, sir – childhood fancy, hero-worship. His lordship's heir to the Earl of Dundonald, who's forever at loggerheads with the Admiralty over one or another of his contraptions – he's an inventor – that their Lordships won't look at. Dundonald's a Whig like meself – ' He broke off to shout at the coachman. 'Take the left fork, Clancy – the shortest way, ye ninnyhammer!'

The carriage was threading a network of downhill lanes whose hedgerows were bright with flowers, but already the dark haze of London was dimming the May sunshine. New buildings and houses appeared at ever-decreasing intervals and below on the right, glimpsed through the hedgerow gaps, the Thames shone dully between unbroken lines of wharves and warehouses.

'I fear this diversion by Cloak Lane makes you short of time, sir,' said Bissell.

'I'll be in time for the Debate, never fear.' Mr Tierney leaned forward. 'You know it's to be war?'

'I'd assumed so,'

'There's nothing more certain now that Addington's out and Pitt's in. I'm a Whig meself, as I was saying, but I'm no Foxite, sir, and Billy Pitt has my support. Aye, until the hour of glorious – ' He stopped, put a hand into the breast of his coat, and looked at Bissell with eager speculation. 'I'm to address the Chamber as representing the Irish members and I have the speech here. Would you care to hear it, sir?'

'I'd count it an honour,' Bissell said.

Mr Tierney whipped a folded sheaf of papers from his inner pocket and began to read aloud.

'We regard it as evident that this country is at the eve of a prolonged conflict with anarchical forces. Mr Speaker, sir, we shall support the Government until the hour of glorious victory. But, at the same time, let not the Government imagine that our zeal for reform has weakened –'

Here Bissell ceased to hear him. He could see Kathy again tomorrow – why hadn't he thought of that? He had two days more before he must leave London for Portsmouth and it was odds against getting leave from *Donegal* to visit Bryanstone Square. Tomorrow he would get a hack from the livery stables and ride to Hither Green. His landlady should wash that little handkerchief tonight. He would present it to Kathy – perhaps ask if he might keep it in remembrance of their first meeting –

The carriage jolted out of the cross-lane into the busy Kent Road unheeded by either of its passengers. The throng of market-wagons and coaches and men on horseback or afoot grew steadily denser as they approached London

Bridge. The Monument was rising ahead before Bissell became aware that his opinion was awaited.

'Magnificent, sir,' he said hastily, 'and most felicitously worded, if I may say so.'

''Twill do, 'twill do,' said Mr Tierney modestly. 'I'd not complain if I had to listen to it meself.'

They were crossing London Bridge now, a snail's-pace progress in a great mass of vehicles, and the uproar of hooves and wheels and shouting draymen made further conversation difficult. At the base of the Monument Clancy swung his horses neatly leftward between two wagons and turned into the narrow entrance of Cloak Lane. The dingy backwater was quiet, no urchins and few passers-by. At the door of Bissell's lodging, a drab tenement suited to the limited means of a half-pay officer, the carriage drew up and the brief but hearty courtesies of parting were exchanged. Before Clancy had chirruped his horses into motion Bissell and Stella were inside the house.

Mrs Widgett, his stout landlady, met them with a sealed paper in her hand.

'A sojer brought this arter you'd gorn,' she began, and then with a little shriek, 'Lord ha' mercy! What a state you're in, sir! Let me –'

'One moment, Mrs Widgett.'

Bissell was reading the message. It was from the Admiralty. In the time-honoured language, he was requested and required to report on board *Donegal* at Portsmouth with the utmost dispatch, and in this to fail not at his peril. Stella, watching his face, gave a short bark. It could have been a bark of satisfaction.

3

Twenty-two years in the Navy had taught Lieutenant Bissell

that post-captains were not cut to a plan. They were as diverse in character as any other human beings; from the flogging captain who delighted in the lash to the religious enthusiast, from the man with no interests outside his sea career to the man for whom it was a trade with too little spare time. What they all had in common was their professionalism, the knowledge and competence resulting from hard apprenticeship under rigorous authority. Captain Pulteney Malcolm of the *Donegal*, he discovered, had mastered his trade without losing his heart to sea life or the ship he commanded.

Captain Malcolm was a portly gentleman benevolent of aspect and indolent of manner, strict enough in matters of discipline but easy-going in all else. His manor-house and his large family, his hunting and farming and wine-cellar, were at least as important to him as *Donegal*, and fourteen months ashore had not diminished their hold on him. England, hoping and assuming that the Peace of Amiens was a permanent one, had reduced her line-of-battle ships in commission from over a hundred to less than forty, and he was one of the sixty-odd post-captains who, like Bissell, had been on the beach during the Peace.

He was on board his ship when his new lieutenant reported for duty (only the second time they'd seen him, confided Horrocks, the second lieutenant) and invited him into his comfortably-furnished day-cabin for a glass of port. Stella, on her best behaviour, was accorded full permission to sail with her master with the sole proviso that she was not to come on the quarterdeck; a ten-minute discussion of the rival merits of mongrels and pure-bred dogs followed; some lists and orders were cursorily scanned, some blank sheets signed by the captain, and then he departed for his manor leaving his second-in-command in charge.

Bissell had covered the seventy miles to Portsmouth by post-chaise, starting in the early morning of the day following his meeting with Kathy. Alternations of rosy dreams and good resolutions occupied the long journey. Hitherto the ambition of attaining high rank in the Service had moved him scarcely at all; his younger brother's rapid promotion had inspired no spirit of emulation in him. But now a new incentive was coupled with a golden opportunity. War with its chance of distinction in action could give a first lieutenant that vital step to post rank which (largely owing to his aversion to blind obedience to orders) had so long eluded him. It was evident enough that this fellow Cochrane must be regarded as a rival, and if he couldn't make himself a lord like Cochrane he could at any rate achieve equality with him in naval rank and – given zeal and good fortune – in reputation. Admiral Lord Nelson had been nephew to the Comptroller of the Navy when he had been made post-captain at twenty.

William Bissell had no one of influence to push him on, though he might count on a word to the proper quarters from brother Austin, now flag-captain to Admiral Troubridge; but with the hope of winning Kathy to spur him on and the confidence in his own capacity which never failed him he saw no need for despair. Nor in his new resolve did he forget Rob Knott's adjuration to keep a curb on his tongue.

There was work and responsibility enough for two awaiting him on board *Donegal.* Threequarters of her complement of 580 were already on board and a draft was expected on the day of his arrival; enthusiasm for the renewal of war was such that there was no shortage of volunteers, most of them prime seamen. But the stores were only beginning to come aboard and the decks were a chaos of casks, bales, cordage and toiling men. Casks of salt pork and beef, ton after ton of hard-tack, barrels and puncheons of rum, powder and shot, sponge-and-rammers, all to be found stowage in a ship new to him; innumerable spares – blocks and spars and cordage, innumerable casks of water (some of which were found to be already foul and were sent back ashore); the perpetual coming-alongside of lighters and water-hoys, the checking and signing of lists and papers, the summary dealing with delinquents who had succeeded in getting at the rum or failed to obey the boatswain's order smartly – these were his responsibilities, and a host of others besides.

The soundness of *Donegal*'s standing and running rigging, guns and tackles, boats and canvas, had to be beyond doubt, and though there were boatswain and gunner and carpenter to look after these he would be blamed for any fault or deficiency. The captain's presence would have taken some of the burden from his shoulders but he was content to be without it; William Bissell was always happiest away from his senior officers. But it meant that in his first forty-eight hours in *Donegal* he got rather less than four hours' sleep, despite the assistance of Horrocks and the two junior lieutenants, all experienced officers.

Hasty snacks in the wardroom were the rule rather than ordered meals. During one of these Bissell learned that before the Peace Horrocks had served in a frigate, *Pallas*.

'Thirty-two guns, twelve-pounders, and stiff in a seaway,' said Horrocks. 'Johnson was her captain. I hear Cochrane's got her now – Lord Cochrane, that is.'

'You've met Captain Lord Cochrane?'

'Not I, Mr Bissell. By all accounts he's as mad as a hatter, like the rest of his family.'

The news of Cochrane's appointment to *Pallas*, Bissell reflected, would be welcome to Miss Corbett Barnes if she hadn't already heard it. Should he write to her? Would a letter including such news advance his suit (which indeed was scarcely under way) or hinder it? This problem was wiped from his mind as soon as he went on deck again to face a dozen more pressing demands.

Amid the turmoil of shipboard activity in port Bissell had little time to spare for Stella. Fortunately the little dog was accustomed to long periods of solitude in her master's cabin and possessed in full the canine capacity for almost unlimited sleep. In *Majestic*, in which ship Bissell had been serving when she paid-off at the Peace, Captain Foote, a tolerant man, had unluckily observed her relieving herself of surplus liquid abaft the binnacle and had forcibly declared that his after-deck was no place for mongrel puppy bitches; Stella's 'ship-training' had thereafter to be completed on the foredeck. She was now trained to a nicety in such matters and resorted to the shallow earth-tray which Bissell had brought on board for her. The first lieutenant's cabin in *Donegal* was conveniently situated with easy access to the quarter-gallery below the captain's stern-walk, and once she understood that the deck was out-of-bounds for the present she was able, at most times, to take short investigatory strolls between the quarter-gallery and the cabin door, which Bissell left latched open for her.

He had, indeed, taken her with him on his tour of the ship from upper deck to lower hold. On this promenade, the darker reaches of which had excited Stella with the prospect of future rat-hunts, she had won the hearts of the seamen (dog-lovers to a man) and accepted with apparent pleasure the fact that she was once more afloat in the kind of palatial kennel she had been born in. Bissell noted also that there was a more willing response from the crew to his often sharp and objurgatory orders after this tour. A first lieutenant is necessarily the least popular officer in any ship; but some of Stella's instant popularity, it seemed, had rubbed off on her master.

At the end of his third day's labours Bissell was able to sleep in his cabin for a full six hours. By noon of the fourth day *Donegal* was ready for sea, and at sunset of that day Captain Malcolm came aboard to the twitter of boatswains' calls and the presented arms of Captain Macintyre's marines.

'Very satisfactory, Mr Bissell,' he drawled, having cast an eye over the spotless deck and taut rigging. 'Pray come to my cabin.'

Beyond the sentry and the closed door he took off his hat

and passed a handkerchief over his face.

'Well, it's come, Bissell,' he said with more resignation than pleasure. 'War's declared – yesterday, May the eighteenth. We're to sail on the twenty-fourth to join Admiral Thornbrugh's squadron off Rochefort.'

'Not before then, sir? We're ready for sea now.'

'I know. You've done damned well. But we're to sail in company with *Janus*, third-rate, and she's still in the Marlborough dock.' He sat down heavily at the table. 'Your report?'

'The top paper on the port-side file, sir.'

The captain ran his eye down the written report, put it aside, and picked up another paper headed *Captain's Stores*. Bissell was wondering if he dared ask for three days' leave. Another two journeys by post-chaise to and from London would absorb his last few guineas, but it would be worth it if he could get to Bryanstone Square and see Kathy.

'Ha!' grunted Captain Malcolm suddenly. 'What's this? No cloves?'

'None to be obtained in Portsmouth, sir. I scoured the town for them myself.'

'Great God Almighty!' The captain stared at him blankly. 'Can't do without cloves, Mr Bissell. Why, man, we'll be on this station for months, and the fresh meat gone by the end of the first week. Meat out of cask without cloves – it's not to be thought of.'

Bissell saw his opening and plunged into it. 'Feverel's in Cheapside keep them, sir, I know.'

'London!'

'Yes, sir. It occurs to me,' Bissell hurried on, 'that a most urgent call I had no time to pay before leaving London could now be paid, were you good enough to grant me three days' leave – and at the same time I could bring you cloves from Feverel's. A year's supply if need be,' he added persuasively.

Captain Malcolm maintained a slightly pop-eyed stare for

several seconds, tapping his fingers on the table meanwhile. Then he nodded.

'Most obleeging of you, Mr Bissell. Your application is granted. But – I depend upon your returning on board before midnight on the twenty-second.'

'That's a moral certainty, sir.'

'Very well, then. And Molucca cloves, if you can get 'em.'

So at first light of next morning Bissell and Stella were on their way back to London; a muddy and rainswept way, for the bright May weather had come to a sudden end. Stella, usually full of eagerness for any expedition, showed a marked lack of enthusiasm for this one and retired into uneasy slumber on the floor of the decrepit chaise which was the best Bissell could find. Bad roads forced the horses to crawl between Liphook and Hindhead, but the posting-house at Guildford provided a spirited pair that took them on at a great pace – a pace, indeed, that proved too much for the chaise, which crashed and clattered to a dead stop two miles short of Ockham with a broken rear axle. A two-mile tramp in the pouring rain and a night at a miserable inn were followed by a late start next morning in a substitute chaise.

It was not far short of noon when a fuming and impatient Bissell, with Stella trotting resignedly behind him on her lead, crossed the mud and dung of the Edgware Road and gained the comparative cleanliness of Bryanstone Square. It was still raining. The manservant who opened the door of Number Four eyed suspiciously the man in the dripping boat-cloak and his bedraggled dog. Miss Simpson and Miss Corbett Barnes were from home. Gone visiting Lady Pomfret at Barnet. Understood they would remain there two days. And good day – sir.

Bissell was left glaring at a closed door. The wild plan of taking horse to Barnet and seeking Kathy there he dismissed as soon as it entered his head. There was no time for that. Muttering curses on Aunt Honoria's *penchant* for paying visits, he trudged gloomily away in the direction of Cheapside, to seek cloves.

Three days later *Donegal* was making out from Spithead, a brisk sou'-wester on her beam, to her rendezvous with *Jason* off the Foreland. The London Mail had left Portsmouth that morning with a letter from her first lieutenant which had cost him much mental toil:

Dear Miss Corbett Barnes,

I was most sorry to find you were not at home when I called on the 21st. I had looked forward to renewing an acquaintance which, to me, means a very great deal. I had also hoped to communicate personally some news of Captain Lord Cochrane. He has been appointed to command H.M. frigate *Pallas* of 32 guns. As to your handkerchief, which is still in my possession, I venture to hope that you will allow me to keep it until I see you again. It will be treasured as the memento of your kindness by

Your devoted admirer and humble servant
William Bissell.

III

Captain Lord Cochrane

1

The driving rain and choppy seas of the Channel were two days astern of *Donegal* and the rounding of Ushant seemed to have brought her into a premature summer. Though it was the middle of March the waters of the Bay of Biscay shone rippled blue under a clear blue sky, and the ship's triple towers of canvas leaned dazzling white in the sunshine as she ploughed on her south-easterly course with a steady wind just abaft the starboard beam. That her sails were so white was because they were all new; for the second time in twenty-two months of blockade duty she had returned to Plymouth for a refit and was now on her way back to join the other four ships of the squadron off Rochefort.

It was the blockade alone that stood between England and a French invasion. The Emperor, as Bonaparte now called himself, had his invasion army of two hundred thousand men ready and waiting thirty miles from Dover, an encampment that stretched for seven miles along the French coast from Boulogne; on clear nights the glow of its camp-fires could be seen from the hills above Dover. All it required was a few hours of adequate protection by the warships of the French Navy while the 1500 specially-built invasion barges crossed the Channel packed with troops. But not one of the thirty-six French battleships was available. They were penned helplessly in their ports – Brest,

L'Orient, Rochefort, Toulon – by the blockading British squadrons, while the ships of France's allies, Holland and Spain, were similarly immobilised at Ferrol and the Texel. It was stalemate, and while it endured England was safe.

All this *Donegal*'s first lieutenant knew very well. It was in his mind as he paced up and down the weather side of the quarterdeck on that brisk and brilliant spring afternoon of 1805, and he chafed as he had done a hundred times before despite the perfection of his ship and the unwonted good behaviour of the Bay. Twenty-two months of it, he thought; keeping station through the worst winter storms in living memory – sails split again and again, chainplates ripped out, men swept overboard or killed by falling spars, keeping ceaseless watch, with the hope of the French coming out to fight now dwindled to a vain shadow – some aggressive action was long overdue. Attack by fireships, for example. Or a trial of the catamarans loaded with explosives which that fellow Fulton, from Pennsylvania, had invented. But of course Admiralty, as usual, would go wholly by precedent; and the blockade of the French naval ports would continue, as far as anyone could see, for ever. To ease himself of these inner grumblings Lieutenant Bissell halted at the taffrail and looked down on a small brown heap in the corner of deck below.

'How d'ye do, Stella,' he said.

Stella raised her head and answered his smile with wagging tail and twinkling eyes. When it was her master's watch-on-deck this was her post, with a square of folded canvas to lie on, and long usage had made her as familiar a figure on the after-deck as the man at the wheel. Bissell, resuming his pacing, resolutely turned his thoughts from the shortcomings of naval strategy to other things.

Since his arrival on board *Donegal* nearly two years ago he had been careful to keep his criticisms and dissatisfactions to himself. In any case, he had no one to confide them to. He was not a man who made friends easily and there was no one to take the place of Rob Knott; among the wardroom officers the only man with whom he discussed anything other than ship matters was Captain Macintyre of the Marines, a rawboned and silent Scot with a passion for botany.

With Captain Pulteney Malcolm he got on well – so well that he could count on a strong recommendation if ever he had the chance to distinguish himself in an action and come near the coveted promotion to post rank. Captain Malcolm was not slow to realise that in his first lieutenant he had a competent seaman and executive officer who was ready to shoulder extra responsibility, and was glad enough to leave to him decisions which Bissell, had he been captain, would never have left to anyone else. He had left the overseeing of refit and store-replenishing to Bissell on both occasions of *Donegal*'s return to England, making off post-haste for a brief visit to his home; so that his lieutenant could not have got to London to see Miss Corbett Barnes, even if the unlikely chance had offered itself in a period so short and so charged with arduous activity.

Bissell had received a reply to his letter to Kathy, brought out with the mail by the *Medea* frigate. It was a polite little note (he suspected that Aunt Honoria had watched over its writing) thanking him for news of Captain Lord Cochrane and wishing him a safe and prosperous voyage. There was no mention of the lace-fringed handkerchief he had begged leave to keep; but he told himself that Aunt Honoria's censorious presence would have prevented any such mention and that, since silence gives consent, he could add to his hopes of winning Kathy.

The handkerchief and the note were in the inner pocket of his blue coat as he paced up and down with half his mind on the handkerchief's owner and the other half on the set of the mizen topsail. Both considerations were banished by a hail from the masthead lookout.

'Deck! Deck, there! Sail on the port bow, sir!'

Instantly the ship, which had seemed to sleep while Bissell paced to and fro, stirred into wakefulness. The men of the deck-watch grouped along the spar-deck and the throng of off-duty seamen on the fore-deck ceased their low-voiced chatter and turned to stare eastward; Midshipman Curry straightened up from his efforts to ingratiate himself with Stella to do likewise; Dinsdale the master and Trapp the third lieutenant came across the quarterdeck to Bissell's side, their gaze going automatically towards the horizon on the port bow though they knew there would be no sail in sight from the deck.

'What d'ye make of her?' Bissell yelled.

The answer came after a pause. 'Can't on'y see her t'garns'ls, sir. Frigate, I reckon.' Another pause, then:

'She's alterin' course, sir – bearin' up.'

'Mr Fitzgerald!' The duty midshipman came running up. 'My compliments to Captain Malcolm and there's a vessel in sight, possibly a frigate, heading to intercept us.'

'I suppose she *could* be a Frenchman,' said Trapp, a stocky young man with a face pitted by smallpox.

'Hope springs eternal in the Trappist breast,' said Dinsdale, who considered himself a wag. 'That's Pope, or as near as makes no matter.'

Bissell had an instantaneous vision of Mr Tierney in a carriage on Woolwich Common and Kathy climbing into it with a flash of slim ankles. 'We're off Quiberon, master, aren't we?' he asked as the vision fled.

'Aye. Belle Ile on the beam and not much over seven miles distant. They're not likely to send a frigate after us, though.'

The captain's large red face appeared, rising-sun-like, as he mounted the ladder. Stella came scampering up at his heels; Captain Malcolm had so far succumbed to her charm as to allow her on the quarterdeck when he was present.

'What's this, Mr Bissell?' he cried genially. 'A vessel? What sort of vessel, eh?'

The cry from aloft came aptly. 'She's a frigate right

enough, sir. Close-hauled an' comin' up fast.'

'There she is, sir,' said Trapp, pointing.

Captain and first lieutenant levelled their telescopes at the speck of white that had appeared on the landward horizon. Stella, after a companionable sniff at her master's calves, went and sat down below the after rail with one ear cocked expectantly. Coverging courses brought the two ships rapidly nearer each other and before the newcomer was hull-up it was plain that she was a British frigate. Wearing all the sail she could carry close-hauled, she came sliding across the blue furrows, a lovely sight with her three leaning pyramids of canvas and the white spray flying from her forefoot. Over-canvassed, Bissell criticised mentally. Three flags soared up to her yard arm.

'Signal midshipman!' he snapped over his shoulder.

'Aye aye, sir.' The signal midshipman, a lanky boy of fifteen, had his glass at his eye. 'Numeral – three – nine.'

'Well? Look alive, Mr Sankey!'

The midshipman turned the pages of the signal-book feverishly. 'Th-thirty-nine's *P-Pallas*, sir.'

'*Pallas*!' Captain Malcolm sounded pleased. 'So Cochrane's left the Ferrol squadron. Interesting to get a look at the hero of Plymouth – eh, Bissell?'

'Yes, sir,' said Bissell without enthusiasm.

There had been plenty of news of Captain Lord Cochrane at Plymouth both times they had put in there. On the first occasion the port could talk of nothing but the three Spanish prizes that had come in three weeks ago, all of them valuable and one laden deep with gold and silver ingots; part of the fruits of *Pallas*'s independent cruise on the northern coasts of Spain. And when the battered *Donegal* had again returned to Plymouth, three weeks ago, her tired officers were regaled with the story of *Pallas*'s arrival and departure a month earlier: Lord Cochrane had sailed up the Sound with his holds full of treasure – 'like Drake' – and with a gigantic gold candlestick lashed to each of his three mastheads.

It was natural that *Donegal*'s wardroom should loudly express its envy. For them, in an 80-gun ship on blockade duty, there was no chance at all of prize-money, while Cochrane and his lieutenants had won themselves a fortune. Lieutenant Bissell's envy was kept to himself, as was his contempt for a show-away who could stoop to such a flashy trick as that of the gold candlesticks.

'"Request permission to come aboard", sir,' said Sankey, reading-off another signal-hoist.

'Make "affirmative",' nodded the captain. 'Mr Bissell, heave-to at the – ah – proper distance, if you please.'

'Aye aye, sir.'

Ten minutes later with *Donegal* and *Pallas* hove-to at half-a-cable's distance, Captain Lord Cochrane was piped aboard. He swung his lean body over the rail with the effortless grace of an athlete, answering the first lieutenant's formal salute with a quick smile and a finger to his cocked hat. So this was Kathy's hero, thought Bissell; a well-enough looking fellow with his brilliant eyes and high cheekbones, and some years younger than himself by the look of him.

'Welcome aboard, sir – my lord,' he said, with an inward curse at the slip.

Cochrane's glance was directed at the deck just behind him, and looking down he saw that Stella was standing there wrinkling her nose suspiciously at the stranger.

'One of *Donegal*'s lesser seadogs, I presume,' said Cochrane, raising one eyebrow independently of the other.

Oh, vastly witty, Bissell told himself. He said aloud, unsmiling: 'Captain Malcolm is on the quarterdeck, my lord.'

'Thank you.'

The captain of the *Pallas* turned to walk aft. Bissell dismissed the little party of boatswain's mates and sideboys and followed him up the ladder, noting as he did so that Captain Lord Cochrane's dark red hair badly needed trimming and that his epauletted blue coat was stained and patched; noting also that despite these defects he somehow gave the impression of being better clothed and groomed than any officer on *Donegal*'s quarterdeck. The two captains saluted and shook hands. As he crossed to the opposite rail to join the master and third lieutenant he heard the frigate captain declaring that this was a most fortunate meeting, and reflected gloomily that Cochrane's deep pleasant voice was of a piece with the rest of him: an epitome of what William Bissell would have wished to be.

Dinsdale and Trapp were discussing critically the details of the frigate lying with backed foresail beyond the intervening blue water. Bissell, with his back politely turned on the conversation of his seniors, strained his ears nevertheless to catch an inkling of what was toward; some plan of action involving his ship seemed likely. He caught the name *Belle Ile* – that was the island lying across the mouth of Quiberon Bay, its eleven-mile length having at each end the channels by which the Bay was entered; channels threading through rock and shoal. If Cochrane thought he could persuade *Donegal* into Quiberon Bay he'd better think again.

'Mr Bissell! Pray step over here.' Captain Malcolm turned as he approached. 'My first lieutenant, my lord.'

'Bissell, did you say?' Cochrane's tone suggested amused surprise.

'William Bissell, my lord,' said Bissell stiffly; he resented that tone and some imp of mischief prompted him. 'And this, my lord, is Stella,' he added, pointing to the dog who had followed him and was standing alertly behind him.

Cochrane glanced swiftly and suspiciously at his solemn face. Then he shrugged and smiled.

'Charmed, I'm sure,' he said lightly. 'I'm no lover of animals, male or female. But your name, Mr Bissell, is not unfamiliar to me – of that we may speak later. For the present –'

'Lord Cochrane has proposed a joint enterprise to me,

Mr Bissell,' Captain Malcolm interposed a trifle impatiently. 'We should, I believe, take counsel upon it. In my cabin, gentlemen, if you please.'

He went down the ladder, preceding the frigate captain and Bissell. Stella, aware of something unusual taking place, scampered excitedly at Bissell's heels until a word from her master sent her to flop resignedly on her canvas bed under the rail. In the cabin Captain Malcolm moved towards a locker on the bulkhead.

'You'll take a glass of wine, my lord?' he said over his shoulder.

'With your leave, sir – no. I find I can think and talk more quickly without wine. And this matter is urgent, as I shall show.'

'As your lordship pleases,' said Malcolm, not without some disappointment. 'Pray be seated, then, gentlemen.'

'Again with your leave,' Cochrane said as they sat down at the cabin table, 'I'll beg you to omit the lords and lordships, sir. In *Pallas* we find it saves time – what's more, you are in effect *my* lord, sir, being far higher on the Captains' List than I am.'

Captain Malcolm accepted this whimsy with a nod and a doubtful smile. Cochrane rested his hands on the table and leaned forward earnestly.

'Now, gentlemen, allow me to lay my plan before you. When you've heard it I hope you'll agree that *Donegal*'s arrival makes every circumstance propitious to success. Four days ago I took *Pallas* into Quiberon Bay, sounding my way through the Teignouse Passage –'

'One moment,' Malcolm interrupted firmly. 'Let me make it perfectly clear that no circumstance, however – ah – propitious, will persuade me to take my ship into Quiberon Bay, sir.'

Bissell nodded silent approval. The shallow waters of the Bay, 300 square miles of them, were fringed with rocks and shoals and its coast was a lee shore with this westerly wind.

'No such proposal was in my mind, sir,' Cochrane said, his wide mouth twitching in a smile. '*Donegal* could get in, I've no doubt, but she'd have the devil of a job beating out again – though indeed Lord Hawke took his fleet in forty-five years ago. However, let me come to the *fons et origo* of my plan, the same being a Breton fisherman by the name of Brizeux. I encountered Brizeux on the first day –'

He talked rapidly and well, with intense enthusiasm and never a pause for a word. *Pallas*'s orders had included a reconnaissance of Quiberon Bay, which though affording no safe anchorage for French warships was a rendezvous for coastal shipping passing between L'Orient, Vannes, and Nantes. There was no ship of her own force in the Bay to challenge her and she had surveyed the hundred-mile coastline within the screening islands at her leisure; noting the defensive batteries on every headland – she had been fired on from Castelli and Le Croisic – the new semaphore installations, and the trading vessels sheltering in the mouths of Auray and Vilaine.

Off Quiberon Point she had overhauled a Breton fishing-smack and made the skipper come on board. Jean Brizeux claimed Roaylist sympathies and had provided much useful information, for which he had been rewarded with a gold piece and promised more gold if, in two days' time, his smack should be at the same place with more information. Brizeux had not failed at the rendezvous and the news he brought concerned not the defences of the mainland coast but those of Belle Ile, the largest and most westerly of the islands protecting the Bay, where the fortified port of Le Palais faced east above the landward shore. There had been mutiny or some trouble (Brizeux was ignorant of the details) among the garrison of the Le Palais fortress, as a result of which all the soldiers and artillerymen with the exception of a few officers and a score or so of men had been taken to Vannes. Transports would bring a replacement garrison to Le Palais on the 18th.

'And tomorrow is the eighteenth, as you know,' said Cochrane. 'The grand opportunity for a raid on Le Palais occurs tonight – and *Pallas* alone is in poor case to seize it. I've only half a crew fit for duty.'

Captain Malcolm raised his brows. 'You've been in action?'

'No, sir. I've scurvy aboard. Add that I've taken five prizes and sent them to Plymouth with prize crews, and you have the reason why I've barely enough men to work the ship. I can muster perhaps twenty seamen, with Lieutenant Frost and the dozen marines who are still able to stand, as a shore party. I was going to make the attempt with them tonight. But I'd be the first to admit it's not force enough to storm a fortified town of a thousand inhabitants, garrison or no garrison.' He glanced at Malcolm with his ready smile. 'You see, sir, why I greeted *Donegal*'s arrival on the scene as providential.'

'Ye-e-es.' The captain pursed his lips and frowned. 'You want seamen and marines from *Donegal*. You propose, I take it, to storm the fortress by a landing below Le Palais, eh?'

'No, sir.' The frigate captain was emphatic. 'For that we'd need scaling-ladders and military impedimenta of that sort. The place is well-nigh impregnable from seaward, as I've seen for myself. I would land a sufficient force on the south shore of Belle Ile, march it across the island – a mere four miles – and strike at the fortress from the rear, a dawn surprise.' He pulled a crumpled paper from his pocket and spread it on the table. 'Here's my sketch taken from the chart. Belle Ile, as you see, is shaped like a fish lying with its head nor'-nor'-west. Where it narrows to the tail it's four miles across from Le Palais on the north coast to this inlet on the south. The inlet is our landing-place.'

Bissell had followed this exposition intently. Despite the bristle of antipathy which Cochrane's presence roused in him he was impressed by the other's lucidity and confidence; his plan, moreover, chimed well enough with

Bissell's own belief that the British Navy should more often demonstrate that their command of the sea made the whole French coast vulnerable. But the plan, to his mind, presented flaws.

'The chart, sir,' he said with a side-glance at his captain, 'would show us what your sketch does not – that the south and west coasts of Belle Ile are defended by reefs extending far out from shore. We have the chart on board here –'

'But it's unnecessary to consult it,' Cochrane cut in, smiling in what seemed to Bissell a patronising manner. 'You are perfectly correct, Mr Bissell. It's on those long flat reefs that the islanders have hewn out their salt-pans. At neaps the salt water evaporates, the salt dries and is loaded into carts, and the carts take it to Le Palais – using a track that starts from the inlet I've mentioned. And a ship's boats may land their men within a pistol-shot of the track.'

'I see, sir. This information you had from the fisherman Brizeux, no doubt.'

'Just so, Mr Bissell.'

'May I ask how Brizeux knew the date of the garrison replacement, sir?'

'He told me it was common talk in Quiberon.' Cochrane made an impatient movement. 'There are plenty of Breton seamen who'd help us if they could, Mr Bissell. Britanny's hotching with Royalists, as we say in Scotland – isn't that so, Captain?'

'Oh, certainly, certainly. There was Puisaye's rebellion in ninety-five, and the other fellow, What's-his-name, two years ago.' Captain Malcolm dismissed the Breton rebels with a wave of his hand. 'But as to this raid, sir. The intention, I assume, is – ah – destruction but not occupation. Our landing-party does as much damage as it may in a limited time and then re-embarks?'

'You have it, sir,' nodded Cochrane. 'They've sixty-four-pounders in the fortress batteries, Brizeux says. We spike the guns and pitch 'em down. We blow up their magazine – or maybe, if we can contrive it, use the powder-casks so as to destroy the fort completely.'

'Congenial matter for my first lieutenant. Mr Bissell makes something of a hobby of explosives and their use.'

'Indeed?' Cochrane's keen gaze went from Bissell to the captain. 'I take it, then, that you agree to this joint expedition, sir.'

Captain Malcolm hesitated for an instant, with the flicker of an eye towards Bissell.

'I believe I may do so,' he said slowly, 'providing *Donegal* is not delayed more than twenty-four hours in rejoining the squadron.'

'I'll guarantee that your men will be back on board twenty-four hours from now, sir.'

'Very well, then. Use as many of 'em as you wish.'

'Thank you, sir. I'll ask for thirty marines and twenty seamen, which I can augment from *Pallas* to give me a landing-party of seventy men. Two officers from *Donegal* – ' He paused. 'Perhaps you can spare your first lieutenant, sir?'

'Of course, of course.'

'I am greatly honoured, sir,' Bissell said with studied formality, annoyed at not being allowed to volunteer his services; Cochrane's smile provoked him further. 'And I hope,' he added with equal solemnity, 'that my little dog may be similarly honoured – she could do with a run ashore.'

He noted with pleasure that Captain Lord Cochrane was for the second time uncertain whether or not he was being treated with impertinence. Cochrane's slight frown quickly vanished, however.

'We're all of us glad of a run ashore, Mr Bissell,' he said lightly, 'and this should be a rewarding one.' He turned to Captain Malcolm. 'This is what I suggest as to the disposition of our ships and men, sir.'

The two vessels would sail in company to a point two

miles south of Belle Ile's south coast. There at four bells of the middle watch the landing contingent from *Donegal* would embark in cutter, longboat and pinnace, unite with the smaller force from *Pallas* in the frigate's two boats, and pull the remaining two miles to land at the inlet.

'I'm not risking the ships, as you see, sir. It's a lee shore and those reefs extend seaward half-a-mile in places. But I've never seen so amiable a sea in Biscay bay and even if the wind strengthens we've sea-room and to spare.' Cochrane's handsome face as he glanced at his auditors was alight with enthusiasm. 'There's a moon,' he continued, 'but the south shore's not inhabited and Brizeux says there's no possibility of the landing being observed.'

Bissell frowned. 'It seems to me, sir – by your leave – that we depend a good deal upon what Brizeux says.'

'If we do, sir,' said Cochrane stiffly, 'it's because we have to. Brizeux, as you must have gathered, has a thorough knowledge of the situation on Belle Ile, and – for your further reassurance – he impressed me as being uncommonly intelligent.' He stared for a moment at the lieutenant before going on. 'I've allowed such time for the landing and the march as will bring us to Le Palais at dawn. Given no worsening of the weather, my first lieutenant will bring *Pallas* closer inshore at sunrise to meet the returning boats. I believe, sir,' he added, looking at Captain Malcolm, 'that covers the main points.' He turned to Bissell. 'The destruction of the magazine will be your responsibility, Mr Bissell. You can provide the necessary materials?'

'Yes, sir.'

'Very well. With your leave, Captain, I'll return on board *Pallas*.' Two bells of the first dog-watch were sounded on deck as he spoke. 'May I suggest, sir, that we make sail in four hours' time?'

'Agreed, sir.' Captain Malcolm stood up and held out his hand. 'And as we shan't meet until the – ah – foray is completed, I wish you good fortune.'

Captain Lord Cochrane returned to his ship. Captain Malcolm, having (as Bissell had expected) ordered his first lieutenant to select his landing-party and make all necessary arrangements, retired to his cabin. As usual, news of what was on foot seemed to have reached the mess-decks before it was announced and everyone from waister to topman was ready to volunteer for a caper ashore. Bissell selected eighteen seamen and two petty officers, choosing men he knew to be intelligent and reasonably sober rather than the brawny fighting-men of the crew; he could not foresee what would happen when they reached Le Palais but that there were wine-shops there to be broken into was certain. The senior midshipman, Fitzgerald, should be in charge of them, he decided. Captain Macintyre, instructed to select thirty of his marines for a land operation against the Le Palais fortress, grunted disparagingly.

'I would I could take them all,' he growled. 'There's not a man but would be the better of an eight-mile march.'

These matters put in hand, Bissell proceeded to give Stella her meal of ship's biscuit and beef and, while she was eating it, to lay out and check his satchel of combustibles. By the time he had done this and coiled the length of slow-match he had procured from the gunner she had finished the food and – unusually for her – had come to lay her muzzle on his knee and look up at him questioningly.

'You'll not be left behind, my lass,' he assured her, displaying the leather strop he used for carrying her down the ship's side. 'Though by the way you wrinkled your nose at him I'd say you were not greatly enamoured of his lordship. I wonder,' he added, 'what you'd have made of Monsieur Jean Brizeux had you been there to get a sniff at him.'

Stella regarded him for a moment longer. Then she sat down, shook her head, and began to scratch it vigorously.

*

2

Above the dark corrugations of the sea the night sky was clear of cloud as the three boats put off from *Donegal*'s side. The moon, just past her full, hung low in the south, giving light enough to show the line of gun-ports along the white band on *Pallas*'s side and the figures of men sliding down the falls into a boat alongside. Beyond the frigate and two miles away the coast of Belle Ile glimmered pale in the moonlight on a black horizon. The wind had dropped to a steady breeze and the sea was as slight as Bissell had ever known it in the turbulent Bay. Conditions for a landing could hardly be better, he told himself.

He was in the sternsheets of the leading boat with cutter and longboat in line astern. The bright moonlight had enabled him to gauge his time so that his boats reached *Pallas* precisely as the frigate's party were embarked and ready; he was irritably conscious that despite the antipathy he felt towards Cochrane he was anxious to win his approval. As the pinnace boated oars and glided in below the ship's side Cochrane's voice hailed him.

'Mr Bissell? Alongside here, if you please. I'll come in the leading boat with you.'

'Aye aye, sir.'

He eased the tiller over, bringing the pinnace stern-and-stern with one of the frigate's two boats. Cochrane stepped from one to the other with the ease of long practice but stumbled as he landed in the pinnace's sternsheets. Simultaneously an anguished yelp came from below his feet.

'What the devil's this?' he demanded angrily.

'Stella, sir.' Bissell reached a hand down to reassure her. 'She's under the thwart.'

'Good God, man! Was it necessary to bring a dog?'

'I thought I had your permission, sir,' Bissell said stiffly.

Cochrane made no reply to that. He turned and spoke in a loud clear voice.

'Boats will follow in line ahead at two lengths' distance.' He sat down beside Bissell. 'Oars. Give way.'

The pinnace leading, the string of five boats pulled out from the frigate's side and headed for the island, the light following wind aiding their progress.

'Will you take the tiller, sir?' Bissell asked.

'No. Steer for the dip in the hills yonder. The landing inlet's below that. Who's in charge of your other boats, Mr Bissell?'

'Captain Macintyre has the cutter and Fitzgerald midshipman, the longboat, sir.

'I've Frost and his ten marines in one, a bosun's mate and ten seamen in the other.'

For some while they said nothing more. The surge of the boat through small steep waves, the plash and creak of oars, an occasional mutter of voices from the boats astern, were the only sounds. Ahead the low undulations of Belle Ile rose steadily higher, bare down-like slopes silvered by the moonlight and devoid of buildings or vegetation. At their feet, but clearly nearer to the approaching boats, a fringe of shifting white flashes marked the outer edge of the reefs.

'I remarked earlier, Mr Bissell,' Cochrane said suddenly, in a low voice, 'that your name was not unfamiliar to me. You have met Miss Corbett Barnes, I believe.'

'I have had that honour, sir.'

'A friend of my youthful days, whom I'd not seen for some years. In the first letter she wrote to me Miss Barnes mentioned that you informed her that I'd been appointed to command *Pallas*, so that she knew where to write. I'm deeply obliged to you, Mr Bissell.'

'A very minor obligation, sir, surely.'

'Not so,' said Cochrane; Bissell, his gaze on the moonlit shores ahead, felt that he was being watched closely. 'When I was ashore last I was able to renew an acquaintance which –'

he paused – 'which I now value very greatly. I look upon you as the initial cause of that.' Again he hesitated. '*Donegal* was in port a few days ago. Perhaps you took the opportunity of calling on Miss Barnes?'

'No, sir,' Bissell said woodenly.

'Ah.' Cochrane's voice was equally expressionless. 'A trifle of starboard helm, Mr Bissell. The entrance through the reefs comes in at a slight angle.'

The white breakers were close on either hand now, their low thunder plain to hear and the flung spray flashing diamond-bright against the black sheen of rocks and water. The gap between the flat reefs was obvious, leading in to a shingle beach where the folds of grassy hillocks dipped to make a shallow glen. Bissell felt a moment of elation as he steered in through the gap. Cochrane hadn't been able to conceal that he was jealous. Then he realised that though Cochrane didn't know it there was precious little cause for his jealousy, and elation turned to gloom.

Both moods were swept away by the recollection that they were about to land on an enemy shore, and at once he was peering anxiously at the uneven skyline that rose dimly against the darker heavens. Cochrane was already standing up in the sternsheets, his questing gaze sweeping left and right along the shore; perhaps his trust in Jean Brizeux was not as absolute as he had affirmed. Nothing stirred except the small breakers on the reefs, and now these were behind them. It was half-tide, and the flat-topped reefs to port and starboard stood out of the water like quaysides.

'Bring her alongside to port, Mr Bissell,' said Cochrane. 'Dry feet are better than wet for a march.'

One by one the boats sheered alongside the reef, crunching the barnacles, and the marines and seamen scrambled ashore. Bissell, his satchel slung on his shoulders and Stella under his arm, followed the frigate captain as he led the long file of men past rock-pools and unexpected rifts to the beach, a passage made practicable only by the bright moonlight.

'Form your men here on the shingle, Captain Macintyre. Two files. Mr Bissell, will you form the seamen similarly? They'll march behind the marines. Mr Frost, take one man and go up to the hilltop on the left of the gully. Report to me what you see.'

It had been on the tip of Bissell's tongue to suggest that precaution. From the shingle a rough track, showing signs of use by wheeled vehicles, was plainly discernible winding up the dale formed by the opposing slopes of two hillocks and disappearing over the top. He got the thirty seamen into rank two deep (as usual, they formed ragged lines to mark their contempt for the rigid discipline of the marines) and told Fitzgerald to see that they didn't lag on the march. Then he whistled to Stella, who had received permission for a free run round the shingle, and called her to heel. By this time Frost, *Pallas*'s lieutenant of marines, was back with his report.

'All quiet ahead, sir. Can't see far – the track goes on, uphill a bit, crossing open ground.'

'Very well. March with Captain Macintyre, Mr Frost. Mr Bissell and I will set the pace.' Cochrane raised his voice. 'Steady march, men, and no talking. – And no more whistling, Mr Bissell, if you please,' he added as they went to the head of the column.

'No whistle's needed when she's at heel,' Bissell retorted.

Cochrane looked down at Stella trotting contentedly beside her master and seemed about to say something more. He held his peace, however, beyond a word to Macintyre as they passed him.

'Marrrines! Marrch!' barked Macintyre.

There was some grunting and stumbling as the seventy men toiled up the start of the track, which zigzagged left and right to avoid the steep glacis of rocks and shale, a miniature precipice, which fell from the turfy rim above. In the narrow glen beyond the angle eased, the grassy track mounting between rocks and hummocks towards a distant skyline.

Glancing back, Bissell saw the winding double file of marines, white crossbelts conspicuous on red coats that looked black in the fading moonlight; beyond them the darker lines of the thirty seamen followed, with the moon striking pallid twinkles from the steel of the cutlasses thrust into their belts; and beyond these again, just visible over the rim above the shore, was the black plain of the sea and the moon's disc sinking towards a path of rippled gold.

The scents of earth and grass reminded him suddenly of the Peckforton hills in faraway Cheshire, where as a boy he had often walked from the Rectory at Tattenhall with a dog for companion. In those carefree days there had been no sword at his side, no pistol bumping uncomfortably in his side pocket. Yet these moon-shadowed hills were just as peaceful, as unsuggestive of violent action to come. No landing on an enemy coast, surely, had ever been so uneventfully achieved as this, thanks to the Breton fisherman's information. His doubts concerning Jean Brizeux had been groundless after all.

They went on, still gradually ascending, the track steepening now and then to climb slight rises of the hillside. Cochrane walked in silence, his eager stride lengthening as they neared the low crest which had formed the skyline for the past fifteen minutes. The pace he was setting, thought Bissell, was a trifle too fast for the men behind them, and he was about to say so when Cochrane spoke.

'We'll halt on the crest yonder. I fancy it's the watershed, with the ground falling away beyond it to Le Palais. I'll give orders for the plan of assault there.'

'There's less than half-an-hour to moonset, sir.'

'The better for our approach. There'll be enough dawn light for us when we need it.'

The track wound up between stony hummocks, black-shadowed. Over them rose the undulating line of the watershed ridge, cleft straight ahead by a deep notch. The moon had now sunk so low that only the rim of the crest caught its fading light, a narrow curving blade of dull gold against the night sky, leaving the hill-slope below – little more than a hundred feet high – in darkness. The rise they were mounting, Bissell saw, was the last one before the crest, and the notch now showed as a miniature pass through which the track ran after crossing a shallow depression where the dull glint of water indicated marshy ground. As they topped the rise the gap of the pass was less than a quarter of a mile away and the ridge loomed close overhead. A twinkle of light on the rim above the pass caught his eye – a star winking a million miles away. Glancing behind him, he saw the head of the column coming up a hundred paces below.

'We'd better pause, sir, to let the men catch up,' he said.

Cochrane stopped and turned. 'Very well. We've time in hand –'

He checked himself. Stella had given vent to a long, loud growl. Bissell stooped instantly to quiet her and felt her body stiff as iron, the hair on neck and spine bristling. Her head was thrust forward and her nose pointed up at the crest.

'If you can't keep your damned dog quiet, Mr Bissell,' Cochrane was saying angrily, 'we'll see what cold steel will –'

'Halt the men, sir!' Bissell broke in harshly, his gaze fixed on the crest; the sky beyond it was hazy – and showed not a single star.

'Because a dog growls? Don't be a fool, man!'

Bissell's hand was grasping Stella's muzzle but she growled again and strove excitedly to free herself. It was no star that had twinkled up there. Brizeux had suggested the date and approach-route – the deep V of the little pass looked like the jaws of a trap. On a reckless impulse he stood up and dragged the pistol from his pocket. It was primed and loaded and he had only to cock it and pull trigger. Cochrane grabbed at his raised arm but it was too late to prevent the blinding flash and the report that echoed flatly between the hillsides.

'Are you mad, God damn you?' Cochrane demanded savagely. 'I'll take order with you for this, Mr Bissell, when we –'

'Look yonder,' Bissell cut in quickly, pointing with the smoking pistol. 'Left of the gap – aye, and right of it too.'

A figure had appeared on the skyline, solitary for a moment only. Something about it flashed, a sword perhaps, and at once the rim of hills above bristled with figures close-ranked, lining the crest on either side of the pass.

'By God!' Cochrane breathed. 'A hundred of 'em, maybe two hundred.' The high notes of a bugle sounded from the ridge. 'Mr Bissell, I beg your pardon.' He swung round, coming face-to-face with Macintyre at the head of his marines, and raised his voice in a shout, clear and steady. 'Party, halt! Mr Fitzgerald, come up here, if you please.'

'They're coming down,' said Bissell. 'On the track and the slopes both sides of it.'

'Yes. You'll be fighting a rearguard action, Captain Macintyre. Please to make your dispositions.'

'Aye?' Macintyre sounded unmoved. 'This'll do verra well for a start. – Marrrines! Ye'll deploy, double rank, with me as your marker. *Marrch*!'

A slight figure dodged between the marines as they hurried to obey.

'Are you a good runner, Mr Fitzgerald?' Cochrane asked pleasantly.

'Pretty fair, sir.'

'You'll do better than fair now. Your seamen are to retreat at the double. You'll go faster, I hope – back to the boats, have all five brought to the shingle and ready to shove off. Away you go!'

As the midshipman sprang down the path Macintyre was rasping orders.

'At my wurrud, front rank will fire and retire. Get back to yon wee hummock and reload. Mr Frost, take charge of the second rank. When they've fired –'

The rest was lost to Bissell's ear in a ragged crash of musketry from the far side of the marshy hollow, the long flame of orange-yellow that had preceded it ranging wide along the base of the crest.

'Enough to make certain of us if we'd reached the pass, Mr Bissell,' Cochrane said beside him.

Before Bissell could reply the flash and bang of the marines' twenty muskets woke the echoes. The shakoes and white crossbelts of the front rank bobbed away down the hillside like rabbits in the dim light. No shot of the French volley had come near them, it seemed; at that range and in near-darkness it would have been a lucky shot that reached its target.

'Present – *fire*!'

Again came the twenty-fold flash and report, and Macintyre's second rank dashed back down the slope. From the further side of the hollow high-pitched shouts reached their ears against the wind, and dark masses at the foot of the ridge began to move.

'Coming across the marsh, if it is a marsh,' said Bissell.

'It's a marsh sure enough!' Cochrane grasped his arm. 'See, they're all swarming onto the track – it must be the only firm crossing. Come on!'

They turned and ran down the track. Bissell realised that he had been slow to see what the frigate captain had grasped at once – that the pursuit must suffer delay if a hundred or more French soldiers had to crowd onto a causeway six feet wide. Cochrane was calling after Macintyre, who was loping ahead of them to reach his second position.

'Get all your men on the track, Captain, and down it as fast as they can go. Post them on the rim above the beach to cover the embarkation.'

There was a short check while the marines scrambled to the track and formed in double line and then they were off again, the two naval officers bringing up the rear. By Bissell's reckoning they had a mile to cover to the inlet. At each dip or twist of the track he stole a glance over his shoulder but at first there was neither sight nor sound of their pursuers. The hampering muskets and ammunition-pouches of the marines made a steady trot the best pace they could manage; but the way, moonlit when they had ascended it, was in black shadow now and its surface was too uneven for blind running. Stella, following close at her master's heels, had to slow her scamper to a walk on the rougher descents. They were more than halfway to the boats when the first fusillade of shots rang out behind them, but the flashes were hidden by an intervening rise and were followed by angry shouts.

'Firing at shadows,' Cochrane panted. 'All the better – for us men – of substance.'

Bissell resented his lighthearted tone; it seemed to him that an officer who had so nearly led his men into a fatal ambush had small cause for cracking jokes. Then it struck him that this was a peculiarly futile reflection for a man who was running for his life. He galloped on. Ahead down the track he could hear Macintyre and Frost urging on their flagging men, their voices rising above the clatter and jangle of the marines' progress. No further shots came to mark the location of the pursuit – no doubt the French were devoting all their energies to overtaking them. And at last, below the next level of the hillside, he saw the dull glimmer of water and the notch of the gully above the shore. Macintyre was roaring orders, deploying his men along the very edge of the shelf above the beach.

'Retire on my order, Captain,' Cochrane barked at him as he ran past to halt on the rim and scan the darkling shore.

At the water's edge, two hundred yards away beyond the slope of shingle, was an amorphous blackness that must be the boats with the seamen embarking – it was too dark now to see any details.

'We want three boats on a split yarn for the marines,' snapped Cochrane. 'Come on.'

'I'm staying with Macintyre,' said Bissell.

Cochrane, already racing down the zigzags to the shore, made no reply to that, nor would *Donegal*'s first lieutenant have budged if he had. He, Bissell, wasn't going to leave any of his ship's party while there was still doubt of their getting safely away.

'First rank – fire!' yelled Macintyre behind him, and he swung round as the flash of twenty muskets shattered the darkness.

Stella gave a short excited bark. He bent to stroke her and straightened himself in time to see the slopes of the shallow glen above briefly lit by a coruscation of flashes. The vanguard of the pursuit had reached a corner of the track overlooking the gully. The marines' volley had checked them there but the others running down to join them would soon make their numbers overwhelming.

'Second rank – fire!' Macintyre roared.

He had again placed his forty men in two ranks to fire and reload alternately. The muskets up the glen banged and flashed irregularly but almost continuously. A shot hummed past Bissell's cheek and he saw two flashes higher on the hillside to his left; if the French followed that line they would be able to enfilade the British position. He had opened his mouth to alert the captain of marines to the danger when Cochrane's shout came clearly through the din of musketry.

'Retire! Re-*tire*!'

Macintyre had heard it and wasted no time.

'Mr Frost, take the second rank down to the boats at the double. First rank, one volley and down to the beach. Fire!'

The muskets crashed and flamed, answered by an uproar of shots and shouts from the French. Dark figures crowded past Bissell and he stepped back to the lip of the miniature precipice to be out of their way. Macintyre, last to move, spoke as he came towards the lieutenant.

'You and I had better be gone, Mr Bissell. A most instructive exercise –'

Something struck Bissell a tremendous blow on the ankle, knocking his leg from under him. He pitched backwards into empty air, falling a dozen feet to strike head and shoulder on projecting rocks and slide headfirst down the gully. He was dimly conscious of this and of excruciating pain. Pain stabbed again as he was dragged, lifted, carried. Dark night seemed rising to swallow him completely but he managed to croak one word.

'Stella?'

'She's safe,' said Macintyre's voice. 'I'm carrying her. We canna risk losing –'

The blackness rose and swept consciousness away.

3

The *Medea* frigate of forty guns was Spanish-built, having been taken in the action off Cadiz in October 1804. The cabin designed for her first lieutenant was remarkable for space and comfort compared with the officers' cabins in a crowded British 74. Its present occupant, however, had neither comfort nor room to move, for in addition to being in considerable pain he was firmly strapped to a swaying cot to counter the frigate's ceaseless pitch and roll; even so, this was immeasurably better than the agony he had endured twenty-four hours earlier when he was being taken on board from the tossing longboat.

William Bissell, as *Donegal*'s surgeon had told him a dozen times, had been fortunate. The only casualty (apart from a marine with a bullet-graze across the shoulder) of the abortive raid on Belle Ile, he had been got into a boat and away out of range with the others before the French could do any further damage. He had been fortunate not to lose his left leg; the bullet had smashed the bone above the ankle but this would mend in time. So would two cracked ribs and the gash in his head and a dozen minor injuries. He was lucky to be going home, said Lieutenant Trapp and Captain Macintyre, who would have to spend interminable weeks in the monotonous ship-life of a blockading squadron. Bissell thought otherwise. His naval career had been suspended indefinitely – that career which, with the vision of Kathy Barnes to spur him on, had become so important to him. And for this he blamed Captain Lord Cochrane.

He had lain for five days in *Donegal*'s sick bay, in a fever which had mercifully rendered him almost oblivious to surgery. When it had abated and he had learned that he was to be sent home with the mails in *Medea* his immediate reaction had been resentment. But for Cochrane and his ill-judged plans he would have remained first lieutenant of an 80-gun ship in high favour with his captain, instead of being incapacitated and unemployed as he was now. At the back of his mind was the knowledge that this line of thought was unwarrantable; but his native stubbornness combined with an irritability born of pain and weakness to blind him to the fact. This morning, as he lay immobilised with but one eye to see with below the swathing head-bandages and Stella slumbering uneasily beneath the slung cot, his resentment was chiefly directed against *Medea*.

The unseasonable calm that had made the Belle Ile landing so easy had ended and the Bay of Biscay had resumed its normal spring habit of blustery gales and steep seas. Hove-to to receive the mail from the squadron, *Medea* had been tossing and thumping for hours, it seemed to Bissell, with each slam of her hull in the troughs sending a jab of pain through his ankle. He longed for the more rhythmic and predictable motion that would come when she settled on her course for England.

Below him Stella gave a very small growl. The cabin door opened and someone came in; his position prevented him from seeing who it was.

'When's this damned vessel going to make sail?' he demanded testily.

'As soon as my cutter leaves her side,' said Captain Lord Cochrane; he moved to stand within the purview of Bissell's one eye. 'I came on board with *Pallas*'s mail. How is it with you, Mr Bissell?'

'Well enough, sir,' muttered Bissell ungraciously.

Stella, who had advanced to sniff at the newcomer's shoes, permitted herself a recognitory vibration of her tail before retiring under the cot again.

'The surgeon here tells me you'll be on your feet again in a couple of months,' said Cochrane with a kindly cheerfulness which the invalid found exasperating. 'It might have been worse.'

The resentment Bissell had been nursing flared up. 'It wouldn't have happened at all had you – ' he checked himself in time – 'had Brizeux been less – um – plausible.'

Cochrane reddened and his long square chin went up. 'As to that, sir, it wouldn't have happened had you not disobeyed my order. You realise that, I suppose?'

'I did not recognise it as an order, sir.'

'No? By God, Mr Bissell, if an officer of mine had said that –'

Cochrane stopped, shook his head ruefully, and smiled.

'Come, this won't do,' he said. 'I was at fault and so were you. Let us leave it there. As to Brizeux, it's an unfortunate habit of mine – I admit it – to treat every man as honest until he's proved otherwise.' He waved the matter aside. 'Well, at least you're going home –'

'My lord!' A breathless midshipman put his head into the cabin. 'Beg pardon, my lord, and captain's compliments – the flagship's signalling us "make sail", my lord.'

'Very well. Mr Bissell, I trust we may meet again some day.'

Cochrane turned towards the door. Bissell, his resentment unassuaged, fired a parting shot.

'And since I'm going home, sir, perhaps I may convey your – um – respects to Miss Corbett Barnes.'

Captain Lord Cochrane paused to look back over his shoulder, meeting the fiery stare of a single eye. The corners of his wide mouth twitched slightly but his tone when he spoke was gravely courteous.

'Pray do so, Mr Bissell. And good luck to you.'

The cabin door closed behind him. Five minutes later *Medea,* close-hauled, was gathering way on her north-westerly course for Ushant and the Channel.

IV

Rebuffs and Rockets

1

Deakin's coffee-house in Tufton Street was no more than a bowshot from the House of Commons. It had been said that an arrow shot into it at any hour of day or night was bound to hit a Tory; whereupon Mr Sheridan had begged that a posse of archers should instantly be sent for. A favourite resort of honourable members when they wearied of the debates, its patrons on this October noon included both Whigs and Tories, and their talk filled the long room with its low ceiling and oak-panelled alcoves. At a table in one of the alcoves three members were drinking claret and gloomily agreeing on the dullness of the morning's speeches.

'The fire's gone out of the Chamber since Pitt died,' said Dutton, Tory member for Honiton. 'Since Fox died, too,' he added, nodding charitably at Plunkett, who was of the Opposition.

'And what we've got in place of it is milk-and-water,' said Plunkett; he drained his glass and set it down. 'By God, there were times this morning when I'd have given fifty guineas to be listening to Cochrane 'stead of Spencer and Castlereagh – eh, Sir John?'

Sir John Middleton, a pocket-borough member who had not opened his mouth in the House since his election, opened it now to yawn.

'Lord Cochrane?' he drawled. 'Fire-eatin' navy feller. Spouts arms and legs. Faugh!'

Dutton looked startled. 'Spouts arms and – oh, you mean his tirade about naval pensions. That was for the ears of the mob, sir. The member for Westminster's a mere demagogue, a fire-eating frigate captain as Sir John says.'

'Fire-breathing, I'd call him,' said Plunkett. 'And demagogue or not, Harry, he knows how to fire off his facts. What was it, now? A secretary of the Admiralty with two good legs retires on fifteen hundred a year while a naval lieutenant with but one has to live on fifty. And by the same token the money paid out to the Wellesleys' hangers-on for doing nothing equals four hundred and twenty-six lieutenant's legs. That shot did damage, I'll warrant.'

'Rubbish, sir,' snapped Dutton. 'You don't damage the Administration with a pea-shooter.'

'No?' Plunkett refilled his glass. 'Then why was Lord Cochrane packed off to sea again as soon as the Administration could manage it? Did his pea-shooter hit the mark when he shot at the massive peculations in the shipyards and the wholesale corruption of the prize courts? The fact is, Harry, you had to get rid of the most dangerous man in Opposition today.'

'Dangerous? Ha!' snorted Dutton. 'The man's a simpleton.'

'Aye – too honest for a politician. But have you considered his popularity?' Plunkett leaned forward and tapped his forefinger on the table. 'The fight with *Minerve* and the three brigs – the Spanish prizes – the taking of Fort Trinidad – the destruction of Dehesme's army – the ordinary man reads about 'em in the *Morning Post* and the *Chronicle* and they've told him Cochrane's a national hero. He's in the place Nelson's death left vacant.' He turned to Middleton. 'What's that ditty they're all singing, Sir John? –

'Success to our sailors that sail on the sea

'Who with Cochrane undaunted
'Wherever they're wanted –'

'They'll fight till they die or gain *the* victor-*ee*!' finished Sir John in a reedy tenor.

'Just so,' Plunkett said hastily. 'The people have taken him to their hearts, Harry. Your government sharps can see it if you can't – Cochrane can do a deal of damage.'

'That's where you're wrong,' retorted Dutton with a crooked grin. 'Captain Lord Cochrane's under naval discipline, which means Admiralty. Admiralty's under Government, which –'

'Which means you can break the poor devil,' Sir John put in unexpectedly. 'Damned dirty job, my 'pinion.'

Dutton shrugged. 'I could name a dozen dirtier jobs that have kept this government in power, Sir John. And Cochrane's no danger to us while he's at sea.'

'No danger to the ladies o' London, neither,' drawled Middleton. 'You've cut short his courtship, by what I hear.'

'The better for him, if it's the Barnes girl you've in mind. She hasn't a penny. Nor has Cochrane, heir to the earldom though he is. Old Dundonald's estate is mortgaged to the hilt to pay for his mad inventions. Though come to think of it,' Dutton added, 'Cochrane must have a fair amount of prize-money laid by. – The last of the bottle, gentlemen. Permit me.'

'Damned pretty woman, Miss Corbett Barnes,' remarked Sir John, pushing his glass across the table. 'Saw her once.'

'Indeed? I was told she never goes out.'

'Gallery of the House, last month. Cochrane had the floor,' explained Sir John laconically.

Plunkett chuckled. 'She must be besotted on him, then. There's precious few women could stand the atmosphere of the Chamber for –'

He stopped as a stout gentleman with a round good-humoured face stepped round the corner from the adjoining alcove. Mr Tierney, Treasurer of the Navy in the new Administration, was a trifle plumper, a trifle graver in manner, than when he had taken two ladies to Woolwich Common in his carriage six years ago.

'Mr Tierney!' cried Dutton. 'Pray join us, sir. The bottle's empty but I'll call for another.'

'No, no, I beg you. I've but two minutes.' Mr Tierney sat down next to Sir John. 'The fact is, gentlemen, I was obliged to overhear your conversation, and when it trenched upon a young woman of my acquanitance I felt I should make my presence known.'

'I trust you'll acquit us of any disrespect towards Miss Corbett Barnes,' Plunkett said quickly.

'Why, of course, sir, of course. Devil a word out of place. 'Twas just that I could no longer conceal my rôle of involuntary eavesdropper. I've been honorary uncle to Miss Corbett Barnes these twenty years and more, d'ye see.' Mr Tierney dismissed the matter with a wave of the hand. 'But in respect to Lord Cochrane's speech in the House last month, Mr Plunkett – the attack on naval pensions – I must accuse you of inaccurate quotation.'

'Indeed, sir?' frowned Plunkett.

Mr Tierney twinkled at him. 'Indeed, sir. Cochrane said – and he was right – that a naval lieutenant who loses a leg in the service of His Majesty receives a pension of forty pounds a year, not fifty as in your version. Forty pounds. You'd lose that much in an evening's play, Sir John, and not turn a hair.'

'I daresay,' Middleton nodded. 'Pension – damned scandal.'

'True for ye, sir. 'Tis a scandal I've had me own nose rubbed in lately.' Mr Tierney became wholly serious. 'My good friend Mr Congreve –'

'Rocket Congreve?' queried Dutton.

'The same. Last year he filched a clerk from the Arsenal to assist his experiments, by name Robert Knott, late lieutenant in the Royal Navy. Eight years ago Mr Knott had his left leg taken off by a French cannon-ball. Clean off – not so much stump left as would make a footstool, gentlemen. And with this terrible disability he's expected to live on forty pounds a year.'

Plunkett fingered his chin. 'It seems, however, that Mr Knott has found employment.'

'True for ye – and he's the one man out of a hundred,' retorted Mr Tierney. 'We count our one-legged pensioners by the hundred, sir, after fifteen years of bloody war, and how many of 'em find employment? Half-a-dozen, mayhap. The rest limp along on two shillings and twopence-ha'penny a day.'

'So, then,' Dutton said, eyeing him curiously, 'you approve of Lord Cochrane's attack on the Administration.'

'Approve, is it?' Mr Tierney laughed shortly. 'In my estimation the man's mad – blind. He can't see the line that divides daring from rashness. He crossed that line in those speeches of his, and faith! if he crosses it again it's destroyed entirely he'll be. But whether or no, sir, he was in the right of it in the matter of pensions and I'm making it my business to rectify it.' He stood up. 'Ye'll pardon my leaving you, gentlemen – I've a call to pay.'

The polite bows of leavetaking accomplished, Mr Tierney came out of Deakin's, settling his hat on his head as he descended the steps, and stood for a moment on the cobbles of Tufton Street debating whether to seek a hackney coach. The day was dry with a brisk air, and though it was the better part of two miles to Bryanstone Square he decided to go on foot. Once he was across St James's Park the streets beyond were thronged with people and loud with the cries of beggars and pedlars, but he scarcely heard or noticed them, being deep in thought. The considerations that furrowed his usually placid brow had little to do with naval pensions; they concerned the vexatious nature of martyrs.

Martyrs, reflected Mr Tierney, were persons who having

got hold of a good cause closed their minds to all else and pursued that cause in defiance of reason; which naturally ended in martyrdom. Captain Lord Cochrane, it seemed, was such a person. In the interval between two commissions Cochrane had got himself elected as member for Westminster and had straight away delivered two smashing attacks on the government, attacks which hurt because they were perfectly justified. No one knew better than the Treasurer of the Navy that the Administration rested upon foundations of bribery, corruption and sinecure, but he knew also that any attempt to sap those foundations would be resisted by the most powerful forces in the kingdom. Cochrane might have been hustled off to sea but he would not be forgotten or forgiven. His career was already in jeopardy despite his fame as a naval hero. Not that Mr Tierney had any interest in Cochrane personally –

Here his cogitations were interrupted by a torrent of abuse from a drayman who had had to rein in his horses to avoid running him over. When he had safely gained the other side of the street his thoughts had switched to Kathy Corbett Barnes.

Over the past twelve months Mr Tierney had not visited Honoria Simpson's house as often as he could have wished; since Honoria had become bedridden, and with it increasingly cantankerous, she disliked having visitors at Number Four Bryanstone Square unless they were doctors. But he knew that Lord Cochrane had made a number of visits there during his time ashore, and was quite sure that (as Sir John Middleton had asserted) he was paying his addresses to Kathy. For the girl to marry her hero, he told himself, would have been the best that could happen – if only the hero hadn't launched himself on the martyr's road to ruin. For he had perceived with growing concern that Kathy, too, was bent on a martyrdom, from which marriage alone could save her.

Mr Tierney swore mildly beneath his breath as he picked

his way across the ruts and horse-dung of the Edgware Road. Kathy, it was true, owed everything to her aunt and now the old woman was almost totally dependent on her. But that a personable young lady of 24 should devote herself year after year (and Honoria could last another ten) to acting as nurse and housekeeper –

But here he was in Bryanstone Square. A carriage and pair with a cockaded coachman on the box stood outside Number Four. Beyond it he caught sight of a man's lanky figure a moment before it vanished round the corner into Dorset Street followed by a small brown dog. Bassett? Bussey? Bissell – that was it, the gawky lieutenant who had been so smitten with Kathy all those years ago on Woolwich Common. He'd been calling on Kathy for sure. An honest fellow, Mr Tierney had thought him then. If this was another suitor, he thought now, he'd be safer for Kathy than that desperado Cochrane. Less attractive to a female, no doubt; but anything to get her out of Honoria's clutches.

He mounted the steps, and had raised his hand to grasp the knocker when the door opened and a manservant ushered out a large gentleman splendidly and modishly attired. Mr Tierney stood aside and the large gentleman acknowledged his polite greeting with a lofty nod before descending to his carriage. There was a scowl on Mr Tierney's face as he handed his hat to the servant; Doctor Arbuthnot, in his estimation, was a fashionable quacksalver who battened on the imaginary ailments of silly women.

Kathy was standing before the parlour fire when he entered, staring down at the red coals. The face she turned to him was (he thought) thinner and paler than it should have been, but her worried frown vanished as she welcomed him and offered her cheek to be kissed.

'And how is your aunt today, my dear?' said Mr Tierney, placing a chair for her and seating himself.

'Doctor Arbuthnot looked in a moment ago,' she told him. 'He said that she must have frequent medical attention and constant care. He gave her a sleeping-draught, Uncle Tierney, so I don't think you can see her.'

'Then I must leave my humble respects. I encountered the doctor as I came in – and I believe I caught a glimpse of another departing visitor, an old acquaintance. Mr Bissell, was it not?'

Two bright spots of colour appeared on Kathy's cheeks and she showed some loss of composure. 'You remember him, then? Yes – he's on leave from his ship, the *Brunswick*. He – he has called here before.'

'To bring you news of Captain Lord Cochrane, perhaps?' inquired Mr Tierney with a sharp glance. 'Cochrane has the *Impérieuse* frigate now, I hear.'

She avoided his eyes and began to speak rapidly with an artificial brightness.

'He told me that, and about himself, Uncle Tierney – he was wounded, you know, and then was in *Powerful* in the East Indies, poor man – he almost died of fever in a hospital in Madras – and that little dog, Stella, was with him all the time and wouldn't leave him. She was with him when he called this morning to – to pay his respects. And tomorrow they're off to Yarmouth Roads to join their ship.'

'Having used their shore-leave to the best advantage, no doubt. A likable young – ' Mr Tierney checked himself, remembering that Bissell must be nearly forty. 'A likable gentleman, as I recall. Mayhap, my dear, you find him so?'

Kathy hesitated for a breathing-space. Then the ghost of a smile quivered on her lips.

'Uncle Tierney, I believe you're fishing, as they say,' she said. 'Well – I'd have told you some day, and today will do as well as another. This morning Mr Bissell asked me to marry him. I refused, as gently as I could. I like him, but I could never, never marry him. I told him it was quite impossible and I told him the – the reason.'

Mr Tierney sat up quickly, his round face expectant and concerned. Kathy was gazing abstractedly at the leaping flame in the grate, and after a moment's silence he decided to venture.

'And that reason, now – would it be that you've already accepted Captain Lord Cochrane?'

'*No*!'

She had sprung to her feet, her face turned away from him. When she spoke her voice was high and strained.

'You may as well know this as well. I shan't tell Aunt Honoria and I've no one but her and you. Lord Cochrane asked me to be his wife. It's nearly a month ago now. I told him no. I told him it's my fixed intention never to marry.'

'But my dear –'

'And so it is!' She swung round to face him, chin uptilted and dark-blue eyes ablaze. 'My place is here with Aunt Honoria. When I had nothing she gave me all I needed – she took my mother's place. Now she needs me, she wants me with her. Doctor Arbuthnot insisted that she must have constant care and it's for me to give it. I'll never leave her, Uncle Tierney!'

'There are such things as nurses, Kathy. Honoria can afford them by the dozen. Let me –'

'No. My mind's made up and I won't – won't change.'

Mr Tierney detected the slight quaver as she spoke the last few words and changed his tactics.

'Ye're talking a deal of nonsense, my dear,' he told her brusquely. 'Where's the reason in a pretty young woman giving up her life to an old dame because she's ailing, and she with all the doctors in London at her beck and call when she wants 'em? Faith, whether it's Bissell or Cochrane, ye're doing a rank injustice to one or t'other, and that's –'

'Please, *please,* Uncle Tierney!' Kathy broke in her voice shaking. 'Don't say any more, I beg you! I can't bear it – I can't –'

She ended in a burst of sobbing and turned from him with her handkerchief to her eyes. Mr Tierney, much concerned, stepped forward but was repulsed with a muffled but imperious request to go away and leave her. For a few seconds he stood scratching his head and frowning at the girl's heaving shoulders. Then, concluding that he had no option but retreat, he got himself out into Bryanstone Square, clapped his hat on his head, and walked slowly away. As he walked he reflected gloomily that the martyrdom he had feared was already achieved. Mr Tierney was a bachelor who protested with some justice that he knew nothing of women; but from Kathy's behaviour he felt reasonably certain that she was in love with Captain Lord Cochrane.

2

William Bissell was less certain than Mr Tierney as to Miss Corbett Barnes's bestowal of her heart. Though he had not encountered Cochrane since they had parted on board *Medea* he knew that the frigate captain had been paying court to Kathy for some weeks before his own shore leave had enabled him to make a long-delayed assault on her affections; no naval officer in wartime could afford to beat about the bush, therefore Cochrane must have proposed and been refused. For had Kathy been affianced to Cochrane she would surely have given that as her reason for refusing his, Bissell's, proposal. So he had told himself, and Rob Knott, in whom he had confided, had agreed and urged him to try again. For that there had been no time – *Brunswick* had sailed to rejoin Calder's fleet blockading the Texel – and for long months he had nursed the memory of how Kathy had looked and spoken in reply to his stammered offer of marriage. That offer had been declined firmly, but with so gentle a kindness that he told himself often (each time with increasing conviction) that she had a real affection for him after all. Between sleeping and waking in his watch-below the warmth of sympathy in those dark-blue eyes would renew his hopes. It was the first thing to come to mind when he woke in his dark cabin on a morning in March.

Normally Bissell would have been wide-awake the instant he was called for the changing of the watch. But when he had cast himself down on his cot fully clothed it had been the sleep of exhaustion that claimed him, his first sleep in thirty-six hours, and he woke from it dazed and slow to assemble his thoughts. It was Stella's whine, not a seaman's call, that woke him; she was on her hind legs pawing at the cot, and shivering with cold. He reached down and lifted her to lie on his feet – it was not the first time she had asked for this – and as he did so recollection flooded in on him.

This was the Baltic, not the shallow seas off the Texel. For three weeks *Brunswick* had been groping up and down the inhospitable coast of Sweden on her independent mission, in conditions which any captain but the pigheaded Thomas Graves would have considered fair excuse for heading back to England. Bissell remembered, with a wry grin, his own pleasure when the 74 had been detached from the blockading fleet and its uneventful patrolling to go on this disastrous cruise; for disastrous it had been from the start. Even before she had entered the Skagerrak gales of unprecedented ferocity had split *Brunswick*'s worn sails and carried away her foretopmast. Northward beyond the Sound she had been beset by ice, fast-moving floes from the Spring break-up of the northern reaches that scored and splintered her flanks, and in nosing into the Oxelösund she had narrowly escaped being frozen in. Escape from that sudden renewal of the winter frost had cost her the loss of one of her three anchors and another had gone in the three-day battle with shoals and onshore gales off Västevik, the first of two such battles. The second, which had brought her within a hair's-breadth of complete destruction, had ended in desperately hard won victory some ten hours ago. The fierce westerly that had sprung up as soon as *Brunswick* had repassed the Sound had driven her aground a league south of Varberg, and only after endless hours of unremitting labour had her exhausted crew succeeded in getting her off. Bissell remembered the sudden cessation of the gale that alone had made that possible, and how the indefatigable Graves had brought her at nightfall into the sheltered fjord which had been his objective. As he could tell from the movement of the hull, she was still lying to her one remaining anchor –

A lusty bang on his cabin door and a gruff shout ended his reflections.

'Eight bells o' the mornin' watch comin' up, sir!'

'Very well,' he called in reply, and struggled out of his cot.

Stella sprang down to the deck and watched eagerly while he buttoned his peajacket and pulled his cocked hat well down over his ears. She was well aware that in *Brunswick* she had the freedom of the ship; though Captain Graves was a disciplinarian he was indifferent to such minor details as small dogs in his ship so long as they did not interfere with the exact discharge of his duty. At Bissell's word she followed him out into the grey daylight and up to the quarterdeck as eight bells were struck. There had been a snow-shower in the night and against the white background of the deck the muffled figures of the men changing watch showed black.

Bransby, second lieutenant, came forward massaging his cold fingers as Bissell topped the ladder.

'Morning, Mr Bissell. Nothing to report, 'cept that it's devilish cold.' He hesitated. 'How long d'you reckon the captain 'll wait?'

'Your guess is as good as mine, Mr Bransby,' said Bissell shortly.

Captain Graves's conception of obeying his orders was, to his mind, inordinately rigid; his zeal had twice led him to risk ship and crew in futile reconnaissances. All the same, Bissell got on well with a captain whose stubbornness matched his own and who tolerated Stella's walking the quarterdeck with him as she was doing now.

Bransby and the duty midshipman had gone, Turrell the master and another midshipman had come up and were pacing together by the opposite rail. Bissell stared round him as he walked, peering into the paling greyness under the mist that lay low above the water.

Brunswick lay to her anchor with her bowsprit pointing up the short and narrow fjord, here – near its mouth – scarcely two miles wide. Half a mile away to starboard the fjord's eastern shore stretched, a long low wall of pine-forest powdered with snow and just becoming visible in the growing light, its dark line thinning in perspective to where, though he could not yet see it, the small port of Kungsvall lay two miles away at the fjord's end. So far as Bissell knew there were no coastal defences here, but he approved Graves's prudence in maintaining full watches at anchor off a coast that might or might not be hostile. For *Brunswick* was a sheep in wolf's clothing.

When he turned at the after-rail to look for'ard the sad proof of that confronted him. Along the snow-covered deck there was not a gun to be seen, and it was the same on the decks below. He remembered the despair he had felt when, the last gun having been swayed up and overboard, the ship had still remained fast on the shoal. The shot had already been jettisoned. Graves had ordered the water-casks overboard – and that had turned the scale. At last the mob of men straining at the capstan felt the movement of her hull and the kedge-cable drew her off. But there was less than a ton of water remaining, barely enough for her 580 men if she began her voyage homeward now; perhaps that fact would induce the captain to delay here no longer than a day. But of course, after what had happened three days ago, he had to wait for at least a day.

From what Graves (an incommunicative man) had told him, Bissell understood that *Brunswick*'s orders had been to cruise up the coast of Sweden and bring back what news she could of the state of that hapless country, whose mad King Gustavus was said to be preparing to ally himself with Bonaparte. The ice and fog of a late winter had rendered the northern ports unapproachable but Graves had managed to gather some information, chiefly from the skippers of fishing-boats. The army chiefs, it seemed, were forcing Gustavus into Napoleon's arms. Alliance with France was not far off. Even now English nationals who happened to be in Sweden were under house arrest.

The skipper they had questioned three days ago had more urgent information to give. His craft was out of a tiny port ten miles overland from Kungsvall and he professed himself a violent anti-Bonapartist. Two Englishmen, he said, had eluded the authorities in Gothenburg and were in hiding in the house of his cousin at Kungsvall. Graves had given the skipper money and asked him to make instantly for Kungsvall with a message for the Englishmen: they were to be ready to board *Brunswick* when she entered the Kungsvall fjord in two days' time. Now the ship was here, a day late because of that shoal, and if Sweden had by now entered the war against England she was in a highly dangerous position.

Bissell frowned as he paced to and fro, remembering Jean Brizeux and the ambush on Belle Ile. That Swedish fisherman could have taken his news to Gothenburg instead of to Kungsvall. Even if there was no ship of force in Gothenburg, half-a-dozen gunboats could make short work of a 74 with all her seventy-four guns at the bottom of the sea. The dull grey light was growing and beyond the leaden sheet of water scarcely rippled by the light offshore wind he thought he could see the houses of the little port at the fjord's head. Would these fugitives – if indeed they existed and had seen the ship – come by boat from the port or from the forested shore to starboard? He halted at the taffrail and raised his voice.

'D'ye hear, there! Lookouts to masthead, fore and main.'

He turned to the midshipman. 'Mr Andrews, for'ard with you and see the jolly-boat's cleared away ready for launching.'

The two Englishmen might have no boat, in which case they were likely to make for the shore nearest the ship. Captain Graves (unusually late on deck this morning) would approve these preparations; there were no others that he could think of.

Two bells were struck as he resumed his pacing. Stella, who had been trotting patiently up and down beside him, was looking up at him with one ear pricked according to her custom, and he gave her the customary dismissal which sent her bounding down the ladder to fraternize with the watch-on-deck, who had scraps of ship's-biscuit in their pockets for her. On her way for'ard she paused a moment to raise her head and sniff at the long bundle wrapped in tarred canvas that was lashed amidships between main and mizen. Gunpowder seemed to have a special attraction for Stella, and the cylinders of the Congreve rockets –

Rockets! Bissell stopped in mid-pace to slap his thigh. How had he come to forget them? True, they had remained untouched since they had come aboard at the Nore six months ago under Graves's disapproving eye, and the captain, who detested anything savouring of innovation, had refused his earlier requests for a test firing. But *Brunswick* was not, after all, entirely devoid of weapons. They had been Rob Knott's idea. Knott, as Bissell had discovered during that momentous leave in London, had blossomed into a competent draughtsman; 'Rocket' Congreve had taken him under his wing and set him up in a snug office-cum-dwelling in Brook Street, where he worked at endless new plans devised by the inventor. William Congreve had pulled the necessary strings at Admiralty and the Arsenal and Captain Graves found himself obliged to take on board one dozen newly-designed rockets and a firing-frame.

Bissell was marshalling his arguments for the immediate emplacement of this forgotten weapon when the captain came up the ladder to the quarterdeck. Captain Graves's broad, stocky figure was rendered bulkier by a heavy pea-jacket. Like Bissell, he was unshaven this morning and the square-jawed countenance beneath his cocked hat showed traces of the fatigue he had endured with his crew during the past days. One sweeping glance of his narrowed eyes took in deck, masthead lookouts, and the shores and waters of the fjord before he grunted a curt 'Morning' at his first lieutenant and began to stump up and down his quarterdeck.

Rigid custom required Lieutenant Bissell to leave that side of the deck for his captain's walk. Instead, and inviting rebuke, he fell into step alongside Graves.

'By 'r leave, sir,' he said rapidly, 'an urgent matter for your attention. These may be enemy waters and we've not a gun left to defend –'

'Pray be less obvious, Mr Bissell,' snapped Graves impatiently. 'And briefer.'

'Yes, sir. We've the Congreve rockets. I submit we should mount the firing-frame ready for use in case of attack.'

The captain snorted. 'Attack – from Kungsvall?'

'They could mount six-pounders in boats, sir.'

The two had paced the length of the quarterdeck twice before Graves spoke again.

'Very well. See to it. And Mr Bissell,' he added as the lieutenant turned to obey, 'relieve those lookouts every hour. They're to keep their eyes skinned for two men. Shore or boat.'

'Aye aye, sir.'

Bissell ran down the ladder to select a petty officer and six hands from the watch-on-deck. It was too much to expect Graves to allow a rocket-firing frame on his quarterdeck but there was room enough – if he remembered Knott's dimensions correctly – on the after-deck abaft the mizen.

Stella came trotting aft from her foraging trip as the tarred-canvas wrappings were stripped off, and inspected the contents with immense enthusiasm and a plain eagerness to be afforded a demonstration of their use. Of this she would have to be deprived, Bissell decided. He had no clear idea of what happened when a Congreve rocket was fired, and if – as he hoped – he was to have the chance of firing one Stella would be safer out of the way. He told the petty officer to take her below to his cabin and set about the erection of the firing-frame.

It was a very simple apparatus. A narrow ladder of fourteen rungs was supported at one end by a triangular framework of two stout poles braced by a crosspiece, thus forming a tall tripod of reasonable rigidity. The side members of the ladder extended at the top in two metal troughs with retaining loops for the rocket heads, and open clips had been affixed lower down to hold the rocket-sticks straight. The feet of ladder and poles were fitted with angled spikes, very sharp, to grip the deck. Elevation was adjusted by simply moving the foot of the ladder back or forward. It looked a singularly flimsy mounting to a man who knew the massive recoil of an 18-pounder gun; yet the rockets, according to Rob Knott, had a range of $1\frac{1}{2}$ miles.

'That's the beauty of it,' Rob had explained. 'The force of the recoil goes into the propelling of the projectile. See you dowse your deck abaft the frame, Will,' he had added. 'The sparks could burn it when she fires.'

Remembering this, Bissell dispatched two hands to fill and bring buckets of water and then stood considering his new toy while the thin snow was cleared for the placing of the spiked feet. Plainly some kind of rocket-drill would have to be devised. His eye caught the crowd of seamen who had come aft to watch the fun and he snapped an order that dispersed them. Trotting aft through the retreating men came Mr Grundy, the warrant-officer gunner, and Bissell, reflecting that he should have done this earlier, called him into conference. Mr Grundy had a face like a hatchet and a voice like a rasp. A Cockney and proud of it, his mind latched-on instantly to the needs of the new weapon as soon as it had been briefly explained to him.

'Right,' he barked, swinging on his heel to face the half-dozen hands. 'Get lined up 'ere, an' smartly. Number orf. Right. One an' two, trainers. you'll 'andle these 'ere poles at the for'ard end. Number three, layer – 'ere at the arse-end of the ladder. Four, five an' six, loaders. Shall you fire 'er yourself, sir?'

'Yes,' said Bissell.

'Right. You'll need a linstock, sir – slow-match on a bit o' stick. – Attention! And you, Murphy, wipe that silly grin orf your face. Five an' six, your station's 'ere by the rockets. Come on, jump to it!'

The rockets had been laid on the tarred canvas, below the rail. Their stout sticks were 14 feet long and the iron case of the projectile at one end occupied 3 feet of this and was 4 inches in diameter. A short fuse protruded from the bottom of the projectile, and its head – Knott had told Bissell – contained tamped gunpowder and a dozen musket-balls, which gave it a total weight of 30 pounds.

'*Nah* then!' continued Grundy. 'Hon the word load, Number Four mounts the ladder an' five an' six bring 'im two rockets which 'e slots into the sockets port an' starboard. Five an' six see as the sticks is in these 'ere clips – right? Four will then dee-scend the ladder –'

'Deck, there! Boat putting out from the port, sir!'

The hail from the foremasthead interrupted Mr Grundy for a moment only.

' – an' all 'ands will stand smartly back well clear of the arse-end. One, two and three will lay an' train as hordered by the gun-captain, which is to say rocket-captain –'

'Deck! Two boats, heading for us. Both pulling hard, seemingly.'

'Mr Grundy,' said Bissell, 'get me that linstock, if you

please. Stand by, you men.'

Dragging his Dollond glass from his pocket, he sprang into the mizen shrouds and steadied the lens with cold fingers. A black speck far across the grey water leapt into close detail: two men in a small boat pulling frenziedly and – judging by the splashes – inefficiently. A shift of the glass showed the second and larger boat some distance astern, three oars a side and carrying seven or eight men.

'Mr Bissell!'

'Sir!'

Captain Graves met him at the top of the ladder. 'Our men yonder, likely enough. That contraption of yours work?'

'It should, sir.'

'H'm. Don't want to kill any Swedes. Not at war yet, far as we know.'

Bransby, who had just come on deck, broke in. 'See there, sir!'

A puff of smoke drifted from the pursuing boat and the crack of a musket-shot came to their ears.

'Mr Bissell, I'll thank you to give what covering fire you can,' said Graves at once. 'Mr Bransby, launch the jolly-boat. Mr Graham – ' this to the captain of marines, who came up the ladder as the two officers sprang down it – 'four of your men in the jolly-boat, if you please. With muskets.'

Bissell slipped on the snow as he landed on the afterdeck but recovered himself and yelled at his rocket-crew to take station. The small boat, it was certain, would be overtaken long before the jolly-boat could give any help. All depended on whether he could bring his rockets into action immediately. And that was impossible as things were – the ship's masts and shrouds stood directly between him and his target. Calling a man to help him, he jumped to the wheel, slipped the becket from the spokes, and put the helm hard over. The resulting alteration in the angle at which the ship was lying was slight, but it was enough to let him see the black dots of the approaching boats through the gap between masts and shrouds. The rigging would have to take its chance. The men with the water-buckets were standing by and from for'ard Mr Grundy came at a trot brandishing a smoking linstock.

'Load!'

There was some fumbling as the loaders adjusted the rockets but they managed well enough. Working with feverish speed, Bissell and the trainers manoeuvred the frame until the rockets positioned on the ladder pointed at the target. Bissell sprang to the rail. Range something less than a mile – and the pursuing boat was closing-up fast. No good trying to get the elevation until he'd fired the first shot. He took the linstock from Grundy's hand.

'Stand clear!'

The rocket fuse sizzled as he applied the linstock. Then, with a noise like the hiss of a giant serpent, a dazzling jet shot downward from the base of the rocket and a bright yellow arc was drawn across the grey sky, bringing an involuntary *o-o-ooh*! of admiration from the hands on the foredeck. The distant sound of a report was followed by Graves's shout.

'Over, Mr Bissell. But in line.'

'Aye aye, sir. – Layer!'

The layer, assisted by Grundy, was already dragging back the ladder-foot to give a lower angle. Bissell saw that the back-blast from the rocket had cleared the snow from a wedge-shaped section of deck and realised that he had forgotten the water.

'Dowse the deck here – one bucket. Stand clear, all.'

One of the shrouds parted with a twang as the second rocket flashed its fiery trail above the deck, and the men in the jolly-boat, which was just putting off, ducked their heads in ridiculous panic. Bissell, gazing from the rail, could see by its straight arc of flight that the obstacle had not deflected it but the trail of sparks prevented him from observing its fall.

'Load!' he shouted, jumping back to the frame. 'Lively about it –'

'Mr Bissell,' came the captain's voice, 'you can cease fire. The pursuit's given up.'

Bissell ran up to the quarterdeck feeling very pleased with himself. A new weapon, hitherto untested, and at the second shot –

'Did I score a hit, sir?' he asked eagerly.

'Very nearly, Mr Bissell – on the escaping boat,' Graves replied drily.

'Two fathoms lower and you'd have got 'em,' said Bransby, grinning. 'Never mind – you scared off the Swedes.'

Far across the dull sheen of the fjord the Swedish boat was receding towards Kungsvall. The smaller boat, its two occupants presumably exhausted, lay motionless half-a-mile from the ship with the jolly-boat fast coming up to it. Ten minutes later the rescued pair, two men in cloaks and fur caps, were being helped over the rail to be greeted by the captain and his first lieutenant.

'A thousand thanks, Captain,' said the first arrival, a tall fellow with a merry eye. 'A close shave – more aptly, perhaps, a close haircut.' He waved a hand at his shorter companion. 'Allow me to present Doctor James Molloy, late of Gothenburg University.'

Graves touched his hat. 'Servant, sir. Welcome aboard. You also, Mr –'

'Cochrane,' said the tall man; he threw back his cloak to reveal a stained scarlet coat. 'Basil Cochrane, lieutenant-colonel in His Majesty's Hundred-and-Fourth Regiment of Foot.'

*

3

'A skilful leech is better far,' declared Doctor Molloy with a mischievous glance at his fellow-diners, 'than half-a-hundred men of war. You'll find that in Butler's *Hudibras.*'

'I daresay,' countered Colonel Cochrane, grinning. 'But better at what, Doctor – killing or curing?'

They had dined in the captain's cabin with Graves and his first lieutenant and were lingering over the wine. *Brunswick* had cleared the Skaw four hours ago and now was out in the Skagerrak, with her 450-mile course to the Downs clear ahead and the favouring north-easter blowing so gently and steadily that *Brunswick* hardly rolled at all although her drastic jettisoning of guns, water and shot had left her a good 500 tons lighter. The claret in Captain Graves's big decanter shifted very little behind its cut-glass wall.

'That,' said the Doctor gravely, 'depends in both cases on the degree of skill.'

'And there speaks medical authority.' The Colonel turned to Graves. 'My companion in adversity hasn't told you, sir, that he's the greatest authority in England on the ailments of women.'

'In Britain, by your leave,' Molloy amended.

'Oh, a thousand apologies, my dear Doctor – I'd forgot you were an Irishman. And yet, since the Union –'

'Ah, the Union,' cut in Molloy, with a twinkle in his shrewd grey eyes. 'There's a piece of work that's brought more advantages to England than to Ireland, sir.'

'How so?'

'Why, haven't you gained a hundred new members of Parliament, all Irishmen?'

'Yes, but you spoke of advantages.'

'What else would you call the acquisition of one hundred lively and intelligent natives of Erin? It's a leaven your legislature has long needed, Colonel, I'm telling you. Let us take an example –'

They wrangled amicably on while Bissell, watching them, thought he had never seen two men more strongly contrasted. Molloy was past middle-age, a small spare man sharp-featured like a lawyer and with a lawyer's penetrating glance beneath iron-grey brows. If he was as learned as his companion in adversity claimed, he chose to wear his learning lightly. The Honourable Basil Cochrane, Captain Lord Cochrane's younger brother, was a large man, fresh-coloured and inclined to stoutness, with a round cheerful face and magnificent black sidewhiskers; only in the dancing brilliance of his eyes did he much resemble his naval brother, and Bissell found him likable and amusing.

The tales of both rescuees had been told over the 'portable' soup and salt-beef hash which was the best Graves's steward could provide at short notice. Cochrane, originally on General Moore's staff, had been attached as military observer to the Swedish army of Värmland until that army had mutinied. Warned by a friendly Swedish officer of the sudden order from Stockholm requiring the arrest of all British personnel, he had left Gothenburg in the nick of time, taking with him nothing but his money and important papers. Doctor Molloy's story was much the same; his friendly informant had been the learned Doctor Horn, Swedish specialist in Molloy's own medical subject, with whom he had been working at Gothenburg University. At Kungsvall lived a man whose wife's malady had been cured by Horn's treatment, and to him Molloy had been hurriedly dispatched in a carrier's wagon for concealment until such time as transport to England could be arranged. A man leading a pony with a cast shoe, overtaken by the wagon a mile out of Gothenburg, had proved to be an English lieutenant-colonel of Foot, and the fugitives had joined forces.

'But the damned Turnips nosed us out,' Basil Cochrane

had ended the account. 'They've as many secret police as Boney, take my word for it. We got your message the day before these what-d'ye-call-ems – Swedish Bow Street runners – arrived, and hid in a warehouse on the quay. I never want to smell fish again, by God! We'd marked down a small boat ready for stealing and were into it like a shot when we saw the ship, but they spotted us. And by God, sir, they'd have nabbed us but for your rockets!'

The rockets had clearly interested Basil greatly, but his questioning of Captain Graves about their nature had brought him no enlightenment since the captain's dislike of rockets was equalled by his ignorance of them. Graves, most unsociable of post-captains, had indeed contributed little to the conversation at dinner, which had mostly been sustained by his guests. Doctor Molloy was a good talker and revelled in controversy.

'Look at your army, Colonel,' he was saying now, with a quizzical side-glance at Bissell. 'Half of it's Irish, and the best general you've got is Arthur Wellesley, a Dublin Irishman.'

'I'll give you that, by God – and here's to Sir Arthur in a bumper,' said Basil, tossing off a full glass.

'And – as the Captain here could tell you – the present Treasurer of the Navy's an Irishman,' pursued the Doctor. 'And I should know, for Sam Tierney's my own sister's husband's cousin. In brief, Colonel, but for the Irish you English would be in a poor way. Our host frowns, I see,' he added, turning a humorously belligerent eye on the silent Graves. 'You don't agree, Captain?'

'I was considering another matter,' Graves said slowly, with a faint smile. 'The limitation of your medical skill, Doctor.'

'To women's ailments?' Molloy accepted this change of subject without a blink. 'Their name is legion, sir. The ladies, bless 'em, delight in ailments, and quite ten per cent of them are genuine, I assure you. Why, I could tell you –'

Here a knock on the cabin door heralded the entrance of a bashful midshipman with a message from the deck. Mr Bransby's compliments and the wind was freshening. A reef in tops'ls and topgallants –

'I'll come.' The captain rose with alacrity. 'You will excuse me, gentlemen.'

He took his peajacket from a hook and went out. At once Basil Cochrane turned to Bissell.

'Now, sir,' he said eagerly, 'these Congreve rockets. You saved our bacon with 'em – came damned near to frying it with your second shot, in fact – so you, at least, can give me some information. I've long thought we could use 'em in the army.'

'There's little enough I can tell you, Colonel.' Bissell, remembering his duties as surrogate host, refilled the three glasses. 'Such as it is , here it is.'

He described how the rockets came to be on board at the instance of Rob Knott and William Congreve and the last-minute erection of the firing-frame. It was clear from Basil's interpolated questions (which, despite the large cargo of claret he was carrying, were shrewd and to the point) that he had studied ballistics and explosives.

'It's a weapon with a future, devil doubt it,' he pronounced when Bissell had ended. 'It puts the fear of God into the enemy, for one thing – and that's a useful thing in any weapon, sir.'

Bissell nodded emphatically. 'Just so. It's long been my opinion that we should use such weapons – rockets, fireships, new devices like Fulton's invention –'

'Torpedo, he calls it. Go on, Mr Bissell.'

'We should use them for attack, all along the French coast. Put every Frenchman from Havre to Bordeaux under threat of invasion.' Bissell, warming to his pet thesis, leaned across the table. 'If we do nothing but maintain the blockade it's stalemate. We need to strike, to make 'em cry to their Emperor for protection. If we do that, Boney 'll be forced to divert half his army to coastal defence – and that's a moral certainty.'

'By God!' cried the Colonel, banging his fist on the table. 'You're the man for brother Tom! I've heard him say what you've just said a dozen times, word for word.' He turned to Molloy. 'You've not met my brother Tom, Doctor? He's the lord, y'know – Captain Lord Cochrane.'

'I've not had that honour,' Molloy said. 'I've heard of his exploits – everyone has.'

'You're right. Tom's the family hero, and a damned fine fellow though I say it myself. Here's to him!' Basil drained his glass and then regarded it with the uncertain frown of a man who is not quite sober. 'Eight months since I saw Tom last, in London,' he added reflectively, 'and then he wasn't himself. Been crossed in love, I gathered. Damn the women! – But never mind that. These offensive weapons, Mr Bissell – how would you deploy them? Take fireships, for example.'

Bissell, nothing loth, plunged into an exposition which Colonel Cochrane followed with an unfeigned interest that encouraged him to further confidences. The Dutch, blockaded in the Texel by nine British ships including *Brunswick*, had begun constructing a mighty boom across the 2,500-yard strait of the Texelsche Zeegat, and Bissell had devoted many an off-duty hour to devising (without any hope of seeing it used) an explosion-vessel capable of breaking the boom. To no one had he divulged this, least of all to the conservative Captain Graves; but Basil Cochrane's enthusiasm and quick perception won from him a detailed description of his contrivance.

Their conversation was interrupted by the captain's return from the deck, and since Bissell had the first watch, due in half-an-hour, he took his leave in order to give Stella her supper.

The little dog made friends with both the new members of the ship's company during the three days it took *Brunswick* to reach Sheerness. But while she showed to Basil Cochrane her customary amiable toleration of her master's friends, it was plain that James Molloy exercised a more powerful attraction for her. She would accept with complacency the Colonel's pettings and strokings and respond by briefly licking his hand. With Molloy, however, who never made any approach to her, she behaved differently, making straight for him as soon as he appeared on deck and sitting down to gaze up into his face. Basil Cochrane found an explanation for this behaviour.

'She's trying to make you feel at home, Doctor,' he said with a grin. 'She knows you're accustomed to have all the ladies sitting at your feet and she's the only female on board.'

''Tis the understanding I have of her sex that brings her,' returned the Doctor. 'You've not the special sense to tell you of it. Stella has.'

'I thought it was the human female you specialised in.'

'My studies, Colonel,' said Doctor Molloy gravely, 'have not infrequently brought me into contact with bitches.'

Rough seas as they approached the Foreland kept the Doctor below decks for the last day of the crossing, but with Basil Cochrane, who was a good sailor, Bissell had further conversations and their acquaintance had ripened by the time *Brunswick* dropped her one remaining anchor off Sheerness. Captain Graves and his two passengers embarked in a fast-sailing hoy bound for London and the Admiralty, and before he left the ship the Colonel gave Bissell the address of the Cochrane town house, Number One Palace Yard, where (he said) he expected to be quartered until his damned regiment hunted him out.

Bissell thanked him as they shook hands; but he had little expectation of ever seeing Colonel Cochrane – or Doctor Molloy – again.

*

4

On 24th March *Brunswick* was shifted to moorings off Chatham Dockyard in the Medway, to await further orders. Lieutenant Bissell, in charge during the captain's absence, knew too well what those orders would be. *Brunswick* would be paid off; it would be a long time before her guns were replaced and she was ready for sea again. He would be once more unemployed, on half-pay, homeless. No – that last was not quite true, for there would always be a bed for him in Rob Knott's house-cum-office in Brook Street. It was a bleak outlook, all the same. He was gloomily considering it on the morning of the 25th, seated at the table in the captain's cabin surrounded by the muster-books and record sheets that had to be reduced to some sort of order before the crew were paid off.

Beneath the table, on the strip of thick carpet Captain Graves kept there, Stella slumbered uneasily. When Bissell bent down to look at her she opened one eye without lifting her head from her paws and half raised one ear; she was plainly agreeing, thought her master, that the prospects were far from bright.

He was forty years old and still a lieutenant. As lieutenant he would no doubt go, before long, to another ship, like as not to another 74 on blockade duty where action or promotion were equally unlikely. And his one possible source of aid in advancement was gone; his brother Austin, flag-captain under Troubridge, had died a year ago. He thought of Kathy. He would be in London soon, with the chance of seeing her again. But could he, an ageing sea-officer with so grey a future before him, propose marriage a second time where he had been so firmly rebuffed? His courage failed him at the thought, and with a sigh he took up a muster-book and dipped his quill in the inkpot.

There was a knock at the cabin door and a junior midshipman came in to lay two letters on the table. Both bore his name, and he opened the smaller package first. The paper was headed 'Number One Palace Yard' and the hasty scrawl took only a moment to read:

Dear Bissell,

Capt. G. rejoins B'wick within three days but don't wait for him or for Mulgrave's order now on its way. Come at once to this address. Action is toward for which your advice is urgently needed. Promise of distinction etc.

Yours

B.C.

Bissell felt a stir of excitement as he read the last phrase, though he felt that Colonel Cochrane exposed his ignorance of naval procedure. He could not, of course, abandon his command without orders. If there was indeed an order from Lord Mulgrave, who was First Lord of the Admiralty, he could only leave the ship when it arrived. He opened the second package. As he did so Stella, who had hitherto not moved from her carpet, came out and stood regarding him with her head on one side.

To William Bissell Lieutenant presently in command (temporary) of His Majesty's Ship *Brunswick*.

You are hereby requested and required to report yourself without fail at the Office of the First Lord of the Admiralty, Whitehall, London, at two o'clock in the afternoon of Thursday March 26th 1809 producing this letter as your authority. The command of *Brunswick* will devolve upon the officer next in seniority to yourself pending the return on board of Captain Graves.

P. Windham

Secretary to the First Lord

V

The Fireships – 1

1

The clock over the archway leading off Whitehall stood at five minutes to two as Lieutenant Bissell turned in through it and halted to show his letter of authority to a sergeant of marines. Delays on the up-river journey had left him no opportunity for calling at Palace Yard; there had been barely time for getting to Brook Street, where he had left Stella and his valise, with a hurried explanation to Rob Knott, before coming straight on to the Admiralty.

The sergeant stood back and saluted. Bissell mounted the steps into the building and flourished his authority under the noses of a succession of clerks, threaded a succession of dingy passages, and was ushered at length into a deserted anteroom whose single tall window looked upon the gaunt windswept trees of St James's Park. He sat down and stowed the letter in his pocket, wondering as he did so whether the 'P.Windham' who had signed it could be the same Peter Windham who had enlivened *Orion*'s gunroom thirteen years ago, the happy-go-lucky midshipman who had had his right arm shot away during the battle of the Glorious First of June. Windham's family was an influential one and it was quite possible. The inner door opened and he saw that the possibility was a fact. The dandiacal gentleman who came in was impeccably dressed in the new fashion of drab trousers and long-tailed brown coat (one sleeve was pinned across his breast with a diamond pin) but his cheerful face, with the ears sticking out in the same irrepressible way, was little changed from *Orion* days.

'Will Bissell!' he exclaimed, advancing with left hand outstretched. 'Welcome aboard this damned stone frigate, sir.'

'A well-found vessel, I hope?' Bissell said as they shook hands.

'Come into my cabin and see.' Windham led the way into the further room. 'Lord Cochrane's with the First Lord in yonder,' he said in lower tones, nodding towards a heavy oaken door. 'This is my office – take a chair, sir.'

It was a comfortably furnished room with a good fire burning in the grate. Windham went at once to a corner cupboard and took out a bottle and two glasses, managing his single arm with the deftness of long practice.

'Madeira,' he said, filling the glasses. ''Member the Madeira at Gib? Those were the days! Here's to 'em, and to the old *Orion*. – But to business,' he went on when they had honoured the toast. 'Lord Mulgrave has deputed me to inform you of certain matters and so save his lordship the trouble of doing so himself – which is my job here in a nutshell, I may tell you. Now I'm ignorant of how much you know, Mr Bissell, of the project we have in hand –'

'Nothing whatever,' interjected Bissell.

'Oh. But you're the expert on fireships, I gather.'

'You're mistaken. I've never used a fireship in my life.'

'Great God Almighty!' Windham exclaimed, aghast. 'But Cochrane's asked specially for you. Hell and damnation! Mulgrave 'll keel-haul me if I've got the wrong man.'

'I've devoted some time to studying the preparation and use of fireships and explosion vessels,' Bissell said. 'And,' he added with a faint smile, 'Congreve rockets.'

Windham let out a sigh of relief. 'That's it, then – you're an expert – and don't tell the First Lord you're anything else, for God's sake. Well, now – you'll know we've been blockading the French naval bases for months, years even. The base we're concerned with is Rochefort. The French have ten ships of the line and four frigates there, in Aix Roads, and Admiral Lord Gambier with eleven of the line holds them in blockade. It's been resolved to attack the French with fireships. Captain Lord Cochrane has agreed – after a deal of persuasion – to plan and lead the attack, you are to be responsible for the preparation of fireships and explosion vessels.' He sat back and eyed the lieutenant over the rim of his glass. 'What think you of that, Mr Bissell?'

'I think it should have been tried long ago,' Bissell said bluntly. 'And surely Lord Gambier has officers in plenty who would lead such an attack. I thought Lord Cochrane was at sea in *Impérieuse*. Why should Lord Gambier send for him?'

'Lord bless you, it's the last thing Gambier would do. *Impérieuse* returned to Plymouth on the nineteenth and the First Lord sent for him at once.'

Bissell frowned and rubbed his chin. 'There's something here I don't understand, by your leave,' he said. 'Is this fireship attack to be made independently of Admiral Lord Gambier and his Channel Fleet?'

Windham did not reply immediately. He turned to pick up the bottle, wagged his head when his offer to refill Bissell's glass was declined, and poured himself a full measure.

'This is not in my brief, as the lawyers say,' he said at last. 'If I'm to explain, I open my mouth wider than a First Lord's secretary should. I seem to recall, however, that in *Orion* we used to call you William the Silent.'

'You may count upon my discretion, Mr Windham,' Bissell said with a grin.

Windham laughed. 'Discretion wasn't one of your attributes. Silence was. And it would serve us both if what I'm to say doesn't go beyond this room.' He drank half his wine and set down the glass. 'You've not served under Lord

Gambier, I fancy. He's religious – sends bundles of tracts round with his Fleet Orders. D'you know what he wrote to Lord Mulgrave? "Attack by fireships is a horrible and Anti-Christian mode of warfare". That's why the First Lord was forced to employ Lord Cochrane, who's not in the Admiral's command.'

'And the Admiral has agreed?'

'My dear sir, he has to – an Admiralty directive. He's to prepare twenty officers for the command of fireships. The matter's become urgent.' Windham pulled his chair nearer to Bissell's. 'Here we trench upon politics. It's no secret that this Government is tottering on its feet – a push would bring it down. We've certain information that if the Rochefort fleet should get out it would sail, on Boney's orders, for the conquest of our West Indies possessions.'

'What – break the blockade?'

'It could happen. An adverse gale to blow Gambier off station – and I'm told he keeps his ships too far offshore as it is – could mean the escape of the French fleet. If it did happen there'd be hell to pay here at home, especially in the City. The Government would fall, without a doubt.'

'Lord Gambier,' interpolated Bissell, 'being a supporter of Government?'

Windham nodded. 'Or Government supports Gambier – if he fails they're blamed. So the French fleet in Aix Roads must be destroyed. And mark this.' He leaned forward. 'If it *is* destroyed, Mr Bissell, it'll not only be the greatest victory since Trafalgar but also a victory won by this Government, which will be stronger than it ever was before.'

To Bissell's mind the linking of the French war with the war between Whigs and Tories was distasteful, and his angular face showed his feelings. Windham, watching him, finished his Madeira and leaned forward to tap his old shipmate gently on the knee.

'It's no good, Mr Bissell,' he said with a smile. 'The Administration's linked to the Service with a chain-cable you can't cut. After all, the result we all hope for is the same. The utter destruction of ten enemy ships of the line and –'

He stopped abruptly as a voice from the inner room called his name, and stood up with a nod and a grin at Bissell.

'Wanted on the quarterdeck,' he said in an undertone. 'By Connie Phipps – that's who he is, you know, Constantine Phipps, captain of *Racehorse*. Nelson served under him as a midshipman. Come on.'

He opened the door and followed Bissell into the First Lord's office. Lord Mulgrave sat at a very large table with Captain Lord Cochrane seated facing him. He was a stout whitehaired gentleman with a genial countenance whose smiling blandness was offset by two small and wary eyes.

'Mr Bissell?' he said pleasantly; and as Bissell bowed, 'Very well, Mr Windham, thank you.'

'One moment, Mr Windham.' Cochrane had risen from his chair. 'By your leave, my lord, I'd like both these gentlemen to hear me repeat what I've already said to your lordship in this matter.'

'Oh come now, sir!' The First Lord was flustered and alarmed. 'Your personal objections have been overcome, you told me. You have agreed –'

'I've agreed – yes. The objections are still the same and Mr Bissell at least should know of them. Pray indulge me, my lord.'

Without waiting for Mulgrave's agreement Cochrane turned to the others. Bissell, who had not seen him for four years, watched him curiously; this was the man who, according to his brother, had been 'crossed in love' – a rejected lover, like himself, of Kathy Corbett Barnes. Was he still in love with Kathy? Impossible, of course, to learn anything of that from the handsome weather-browned face just now so sternly set. He noticed again the patrician air of authority that Cochrane wore so carelessly. Doubtless it was a natural trait in one who would one day be tenth Earl of

Dundonald, but it was probably one of the things (thought Bissell) that stirred his old bristle of dislike.

'I wish you to know, gentlemen,' Cochrane was saying, 'first, that I enter this project determined to succeed in it, and second, that I do so under protest. I've represented to Lord Mulgrave that Admiral Lord Gambier, who has a hundred capable officers at his disposal, must inevitably resent the command being given to a junior captain from outside his squadron. When I was summoned to the Admiralty – only three days after *Impérieuse* came into Plymouth – I was told that my advice was required as to whether a fireship attack was practicable.'

'And so it was,' the First Lord interrupted a trifle impatiently. 'You were in Aix Roads less than three years ago and no one knows them better than you.'

'Just so, my lord,' returned Cochrane drily. 'But having given my opinion that Lord Gambier could use fireships there with every chance of success, I was then informed that I myself was to plan and lead the attack. I declined, on the grounds I've told you of, gentlemen. Lord Mulgrave has assured me that all will be made right with Lord Gambier, that the destruction of a French fleet depends upon my acceptance of this command, and finally – ' his mouth twitched in a faint grin – 'that the Board of Admiralty cannot listen to further refusal or delay. I've therefore withdrawn my opposition and shall obey my orders to the best of my ability. I've nothing more to say, my lord.'

'Then perhaps I may speak, sir,' Mulgrave said, assuming a spurious jocularity. 'And I'll remind you that you demanded *carte blanche* for your preparations and that I freely gave it. For time is of the utmost importance in this matter. Mr Bissell!'

'My lord?'

'You have been recommended as an officer fully capable of fitting-out fireships and explosion-vessels. How long will it take you to prepare twenty fireships?'

'With the hulls immediately available, my lord?'

Mulgrave nodded. 'And the Arsenal at your disposal.'

Bissell had to think fast, but he had years of night-watch calculation and off-duty planning to help him and he had his answer ready in a few seconds.

'Not less than seven days, my lord, not more than ten.'

The First Lord frowned and looked at Cochrane. 'They'll have to assemble in the Downs. They won't be off Rochefort until the middle of April. We must do better than that.'

'I fear we can't, my lord,' the frigate captain said firmly. 'Mr Bissell's estimate is unlikely to be wrong. However, I submit that *Impérieuse* should report to Lord Gambier's fleet as soon as possible. If I start for Plymouth on Saturday she can be ready for sea by the twenty-ninth.'

'Very well,' Mulgrave said resignedly. 'You'll carry the Board's instructions to the Admiral. I'll send them round to Palace Yard this evening.' He glanced at Windham. 'I think that's all?'

'Authorities for Mr Bissell, my lord,' Windham said quickly. 'To Director of Arsenal and Captain of Dockyard at Chatham.'

'Prepare them, if you please, and send them to – you have an address in London, Mr Bissell?'

'In Brook Street, my lord. Number seventeen.'

'Mr Bissell will, however, spend today at Palace Yard,' Cochrane put in. 'And possibly most of tonight,' he added. 'There's a deal of preliminary work to be done.'

'Then I shall detain you no longer,' said the First Lord. 'Should you encounter any obstacle, Mr Bissell, you will notify me at once.' He stood up. 'One last word, gentlemen. Much – very much – now depends upon you. The Admiralty is bent on destroying that fleet before it can get out to the West Indies. That is all.'

Bissell had time only for a nod and a grin at Peter Windham and then he was out of the room and following Cochrane's long stride down the passage.

'My carriage, in the courtyard,' the captain flung over his shoulder as they went.

It was a closed carriage with a chipped and faded coat-of-arms on the door. Bissell climbed in after Cochrane, the coachman touched-up his two horses, and they rattled over the cobbles and out into Whitehall. Cochrane spoke abruptly, after a brief silence.

'You were to have come direct to Palace Yard. I needed to discuss matters with you before seeing the First Lord.'

Bissell, sitting opposite him with his back to the coachman, stiffened. 'Colonel Cochrane's note arrived simultaneously with Lord Mulgrave's order,' he said shortly. 'The order allowed me no time.'

Cochrane made no reply to this. He seemed to have fallen into a frowning abstraction which lasted for a minute or two before he spoke again, with the same abruptness.

'Lord Mulgrave sent for you at my request. My brother assures me you're equal to the task. Can you do it?'

'I shall do my best, sir.'

'That's no answer. Can you do it?'

'I can!' Bissell replied harshly.

Again Cochrane made no comment. There was another silence while the carriage clattered and swerved and the cries of the street mingled with the coachman's shouts of 'Clear the way, there!'. Then Cochrane leaned forward and lightly touched his companion's knee.

'You must excuse me, Mr Bissell,' he said evenly. 'This matter weighs heavily upon me – too heavily, perhaps. I've undertaken it against my will, and I foresee trouble ahead. But I'm resolved to succeed at all costs and there must be no mistakes. You understand?'

'I understand, sir,' said Bissell stolidly.

The carriage swung round a corner and drew up before the decaying portico of Number One Palace Yard.

*

2

The Earl of Dundonald's town house was very different from Rob Knott's neat dwelling in Brook Street, which was kept snug and spotless by Rob's housekeeper Mrs Odger. Here – while the Earl was at the family mansion of Culross Abbey in Scotland – there were three servants, but no tidiness. As Bissell discovered in the course of the eleven hours he spent in Palace Yard, half the rooms in the house had been adapted for Lord Dundonald's multifarious experiments; which, as they included researches into coal-tar derivatives and anti-fouling paints for ships, had left those rooms uninhabitable. The big dining-room, however, was handsomely furnished and had a blazing fire in the wide fireplace, from in front of which Basil Cochrane advanced to give Bissell a much warmer welcome than his brother had given.

'How went the day with Mulgrave?' he demanded as they shook hands. '*Tout va bien*, as the Frogs say? You'll be ready for a drink, I'll be bound. I'll tell –'

'Later.' The captain tossed his hat onto a chair. 'I want to get under way with our planning.'

'Damn it, Tom, we've got to eat and drink.'

'Tell Davie to bring sherry and sandwiches at four bells – two o'clock. And when you've done that, pray bring the chart you'll find on the chest in my room.' As Basil departed Cochrane turned quickly to Bissell. 'You were in *Brunswick* on the Texel blockade, Mr Bissell. The Dutch had rigged a boom. You designed an explosion-vessel to break that boom, though it was never used. Is that correct?'

'Quite correct, sir.'

'Do you know the boom's construction?'

'By hearsay, sir. It wasn't *Brunswick*'s boat that made the reconnaissance. Heavy timber baulks secured ten feet apart with two-inch chain cable and moored with thirty-inch hemp.'

Cochrane stared at him unseeing. 'Yes. Even a seventy-four would be brought up all-standing. Your explosion-vessel would break it?'

'That's a moral certainty, sir – if she was properly directed and placed. Even if she went up well short of the boom there's a good chance she'd break it. There's a boom in this case, then, sir?'

'I don't know – and I don't suppose Lord Gambier knows, either. There's been no mention of one in his dispatches, the First Lord told me. But – ah!' he interrupted himself as his brother came in carrying a rolled chart. 'Now we can see. On the table with it, Basil, and hold that end down. This is a captured French chart, Bissell. The marked soundings are mine, taken when I was there in *Pallas* in April eighteen-oh-six. Now – lay your mind to this.'

He was a different man, Bissell thought, from the cold and distant gentleman of an hour ago. His lean face was flushed with enthusiasm and his eyes shone with a curious brilliance as he brought the lines and figures of the chart to life in vivid explanation. Here was the pretty bolt-hole that Gambier was watching to no purpose, a bay – not unlike Quiberon – with its mouth mostly covered by the Isle d'Oléron, twenty miles long. No entrance south of that island, but north of it an outer bay, the Basque Roads, from which the inner bay called the Aix Roads could be gained between the Isle d'Aix on the east and the big Boyart shoal on the west – a passage nearly two miles wide at high water. The French fleet, Admiral Allemand in command, lay in the Aix Roads off the difficult estuary of the Charente where the naval base of Rochefort stood.

'Fortifications marked here,' put in Basil, stabbing the Isle d'Aix with a forefinger. 'If they've artillery in 'em your two-mile entrance is barred.'

'Gambier's last report said they were dismantled and

under reconstruction,' Cochrane said. 'If only Nelson were alive and in Gambier's place! Long ere this he'd have taken his ships in, line ahead, and we'd have had another Nile victory.' He turned to Bissell. 'If you had a fleet anchored in Aix Roads, Bissell, and an enemy fleet outside – if you wanted to make it as secure as possible from attack – what would you do?'

'Rig a boom, sir,' Bissell replied without hesitation. 'Here – ' he pointed – 'between the three-fathom depths off the Boyart shoal and the Isle d'Aix.'

'Precisely. And Allemand – I know a lot about him – is a thoroughgoing seaman. It's a thousand to one he's got a boom there, and it'll be as massive as the one your Dutch friends rigged. We go ahead on the explosion-vessel.' Cochrane released his end of the chart and it rolled itself up. 'Let's clear the deck and get to work. You have your explosive plans with you?'

'I have them in my head, sir.'

'Very well. And – by your leave – we'll drop the 'sirs' while we're in this house. Basil, find paper, pen, and ink. You'll play secretary, if you please.'

'I'll play anything so long as I command the guns when we come to your damned Aix Roads,' returned Basil as he departed once more.

'Is Colonel Cochrane coming with us?' asked Bissell.

Cochrane laughed. 'Can't keep him away. I've promised he can command *Impérieuse*'s starboard guns. He's a volunteer, of course, but he knows something of gunnery.' He glanced at the clock on the overmantel. 'We'll have an hour at it and then break for refreshments. Draw up a chair.'

Basil came back with his secretarial equipment and the three sat down at the table.

'The explosion-vessel first,' Cochrane said. 'What hull do you need?'

'Five hundred tons or thereabouts.'

Cochrane's brows drew together. 'The size of a sixth-rate?

But never mind,' he added instantly. 'We must have it. A small converted transport would serve and the First Lord shall be applied to before I leave tomorrow. What goes into her?'

'The floor of the hull must be strengthened – logs in close contact and lashed together, wedged firmly and the crevices filled with sand. That's to afford resistance to the explosion and render it more effective. Fifteen hundred barrels of gunpowder put into larger casks, the casks close-set on end and bound round with cables –'

'Slow march, there!' Basil appealed, his quill scratching furiously. '"Bound round with cables" –'

'And compressed with sand and wedges. Above these –'

Bissell made his exposition without faltering though he was under a certain stress. He had his requirements and quantities clear in his mind but he was conscious of Cochrane's intense, almost fierce, critical attention. It was merely natural that the officer responsible for such an enterprise as this should monitor the plans of a subordinate with the utmost care but he resented it all the same.

'Two fuses,' he finished, 'slow-match to be cut according to time required, and port-fires to light them.' He hesitated for a moment. 'If this boom is where we think it to be –'

'It is. You may depend upon it.'

'Well, then, according to your chart it'll be less than a mile from the outermost French ships. My explosion-vessel will make – quite a show. And the French'll see it.' Bissell was remembering the blazing brig at Port Louis nine years ago. 'If the wind favours fireships Allemand's fleet's on a lee shore. Congreve rockets would do nothing towards the breaking of the boom, but if we were to place, say, one hundred rockets in the explosion-vessel in addition –'

'By God!' cried Basil, dashing down his pen. 'That'd put the fear of death into the Frogs! Two were enough for me, Tom, as I've told you.'

'An excellent plan, Bissell,' said his brother more calmly.

'As you no doubt realise, half the value of a fireship attack is the terror it inspires in the enemy. Anything that can add to that aids our purpose.'

Basil took up his quill. 'One hundred Congreve rockets.' He looked up. 'Your friend Robert Knott might lend us a hand there. I called at Brook Street and made his acquaintance three days ago – a damned fine fellow, and William Congreve thinks the world of him. He was telling me –'

'And you can tell us some other time. The canvas and running rigging of this explosion-vessel need consideration.' Cochrane looked at Bissell. 'You must see to it that she's rigged for handling by six men only – running free, of course. I've the shipyard plan of *Pallas*, hull and cordage, on the wall of my room. That will show you what's needed.'

Bissell followed him out of the dining-room and up a wide staircase. The frigate captain's room was small and plainly furnished. A truckle-bed stood against one wall and above it was fastened a large and detailed plan of his old ship. On a small table beside the bed was a miniature framed in red morocco leather that drew Bissell's attention; it was a water-colour of a girl. Cochrane intercepted his glance and their eyes met for an instant before he turned abruptly away and set his knee on the bed.

'Mark this carefully,' he said peremptorily, using a forefinger as a pointer. 'Courses on main and mizen are all that's needed but the sheets must be led –'

The matter of fairleads for the sheets was dealt with, and the stowage of explosives on deck, the positioning of the fuses, even the line and shackles to be used for lashing the helm before abandoning ship. Bissell felt some resentment; all this could safely have been left to him. But in spite of it (and though part of his mind was distracted by the presence of Kathy Barnes's picture on the bedside table) he had to admire the minute attention to detail that left nothing to chance. Cochrane seemed to divine his thoughts.

'You realise, of course, that I'm taking this vessel into action myself,' he said as they descended the staircase. 'It may be immediately on her arrival off Rochefort. I must be sure that all will be ready, and precisely as I've planned, when I set foot on board.'

'It will be,' Bissell said stiffly. 'I beg leave,' he added in the same tone, 'to volunteer as one of her crew.'

'Indeed? But I had already assumed that you'd sail in her.'

The hinted surprise that he should have thought himself free to evade danger stung Bissell.

'You've said no word of that!' he began hotly. 'How should I know –'

He was interrupted, as they re-entered the dining-room, by Colonel Cochrane. Basil had already started on the copying of his first list and looked up to demand when he was going to get a drink.

'At four bells and not before,' said his brother shortly. 'Belay that and take a fresh sheet. Fireships – square-rigged, Bissell, naturally.'

'Brigs of medium tonnage.'

'Very well. We'll go ahead on that.'

They went ahead. Basil's lists grew into a small pile as the fingers of the clock on the overmantel moved on. At two the servant Davie, a gaunt Scotsman, brought wine and sandwiches and was told by Basil to bring as many sandwiches again and spread more mustard on 'em. On into the afternoon they worked, finishing at last with the details of explosive cargoes and passing to other matters wherein – once more – Bissell had to admit Cochrane's miraculous grasp of every requirement large or small. These things, he told himself, would not have been omitted by William Bissell; he would have dealt with them as they cropped up during the busy week ahead. But Thomas Cochrane had them at the tips of his long fingers. The little convoy that was soon to sail from the Downs with its deadly cargo would have an escort for the voyage down Channel. The escort must be prepared to take on board the skeleton crews from the brig-fireships when they reached the Fleet. Admiralty would see to that but a memorandum to the First Lord – 'note that down, Basil' – would assure it. Careful waterproofing of the fireships' cargoes must be rigged and checked. Victualling for the convoy crews must be specially indented for. And so on. It was evening, and a large and ugly oil-lamp of the Earl's devising had been lit, when Cochrane announced that all had been done that paper planning could achieve.

'For the rest I must rely on you,' he told Bissell, frowning. 'I wish to God I could handle it myself.'

Bissell reddened. 'You may depend on me,' he said harshly.

'I have to, Mr Bissell.' Cochrane stood up, a little wearily. 'That's all, I think.'

'But Mr Bissell will sup with us, of course,' Basil said.

Bissell hastily declined. He was expected at Brook Street, he said; the night was clear and the walk would do him good.

'The carriage will take you there,' Cochrane said sharply. 'You'll please to bear in mind, Mr Bissell, that you have a formidable task before you and little time for its performance. You will turn in early and make an early start for Chatham tomorrow morning.'

Bissell crushed down unreasoning resentment. 'Aye aye, sir.'

'I'll tell Harry to put the horses to.' The frigate captain paused halfway to the door. 'You'll have no time for visiting in London, Mr Bissell.'

He turned away hurriedly, as if he wished those last words unsaid, and went out. Basil stared after him a moment and then turned to Bissell with an apologetic air.

'Tom's – not himself these days,' he said with less than his usual assurance. 'It's that damned girl. She refused him and he hasn't got over it. The Corbett Barnes girl, y'know.'

'He's not asked her a second time?' Bissell ventured.

'Nor he won't, if I know Tom. Too devilish proud.' Basil shot a glance at him. 'A man might be forgiven for guessing that you're interested in that quarter.'

'Miss Barnes refused my own offer,' Bissell said shortly.

'Ha. I see. Well, you never know how love'll take a fellow, in my experience. There's not an ounce of dog-in-the-manger in Tom, in the ordinary way –'

Further confidences were cut short by the return of his brother to say that the carriage would be at the door in two minutes.

The Dundonald equipage, its smoky lanthorns flaring, jolted through the streets towards Rob Knott's lodging with Bissell and his sheaf of lists and duplicate copies. Its occupant was able, for the first time that day, to thrust the fireship expedition from his tired mind and dream of its possible results. *The greatest victory since Trafalgar*, Windham had said. If it succeeded, that was; but Cochrane would succeed. For all his stubborn antipathy towards the man Bissell felt sure of that. When the story was told Cochrane would be the national hero, a second Nelson, but he, William Bissell, would come in for a share of the glory. Promotion, of course. A knighthood even. A name to be remembered down the ages. With these he could feel assurance enough to present himself as Kathy's suitor. And if Basil's estimate of his brother's pride was accurate he would have no rival there. With a clatter and jangle the carriage drew up before Rob's house.

Stella welcomed him with rejoicing and Rob with cold beef and ale. As he ate he gave Rob a succinct account of the day's happenings which greatly excited his friend and stirred him to unusual loquacity. Bissell would have liked to extend their talk far into the night; but he was dead tired and glad to go up with Stella to their sleeping-quarters.

When he had settled Stella into the blanket-lined box Rob

had provided at the foot of his bed he stooped to let her lick his cheek; a customary exchange of sentiments which he kept secret even from Rob. Contrary to custom, however, Stella did not at once perform her ritual three revolutions before curling up ready for sleep. Instead, she remained sitting upright, her head cocked to one side and her brown eyes questioning him anxiously. He stroked the rough little head reassuringly.

'Oh, you shall come with me, never fear,' he told her. 'We'll sink or swim together in the Aix Roads, my lass. But there's a vast amount of work to be done first.'

Just how vast that amount was Bissell only realised when, seven days later, he could look back on the hardest week's work of his arduous life.

3

Sitting in the sternsheets of *Mediator*'s cutter, Bissell stared across the grey-green hurrying waves at the dark line of the French coast four miles away to port. Turning, he looked astern to the two groups of vessels hove-to within half-a-mile of each other: the eleven great ships of the Fleet with *Caledonia*, Admiral Lord Gambier's flagship, distinguishable by her three decks; and the cluster of much smaller vessels – the twenty fireships, the explosion-vessel, and the frigate *Mediator* in which he had voyaged from England with his convoy.

Ahead of the cutter and to starboard the low outline of the land barred the horizon, for she was well inside the narrowing entrance of the Basque Roads and he could make out the squat shape of the Isle d'Aix that guarded the inner anchorage of the Aix Roads. The island was on the cutter's port bow. She was heading for a solitary frigate nearer at hand, lying to her anchor close to an area of paler-hued water which Bissell knew must be the Boyart shoal. This was *Impérieuse*, Captain Lord Cochrane's frigate. It was early afternoon on 10th April.

Stella, crouched on the bottom-boards behind his legs, nudged him gently with her nose and he reached down a hand to give her a reassuring pat. All was going well. The strenuous week of preparation, the uneventful passage round Ushant and down the Bay, were safely and successfully behind him and the action he had so long looked forward to very close ahead. Cochrane, Bissell remembered, had lamented that Nelson hadn't been here to take his fleet into Aix Roads and destroy the French as he had done at the Nile; but the Nile had cost England a thousand casualties and left Nelson's ships so battered that it was months before they were seaworthy again. Very soon now the method of attack he had advocated all his sea-life would be put to the test, and he was confident of its success. A French fleet would be destroyed without damage to a single English ship of any value, and with the lives of only a few dozen officers and men at risk. And not only Lord Gambier and Lord Cochrane, but Lieutenant William Bissell also, would have their names in the history-books of the future.

The flagship's signal as the convoy approached had summoned Captain Wooldridge of the *Mediator* to report on board, and Wooldridge had brought back orders for Lieutenant Bissell to join *Impérieuse* without delay. As the cutter came alongside below the frigate's single row of gunports Bissell was mentally framing the words of his report to her captain. When he climbed to her deck, with Stella in her 'boarding-harness' slung on his shoulders, it was David Mapleton, Cochrane's first lieutenant, who was there to greet him with a smile and a handshake and a friendly pat for Stella.

'I'm damned glad to see you, Mr Bissell, and that's an understatement,' he said; his round face and snub nose made him look younger than his years. 'And your lady friend too.'

'Stella's allowed on board, then?' said Bissell, setting her down.

'She's as welcome as wine in Hades, sir. Tray, Haswell's terrier, was swept overboard in a gale four days ago.'

Haswell, the grizzled second lieutenant, was formally introduced to Stella and her master and then departed to see Bissell's dunnage hoisted aboard and taken to his cabin.

'Lord Cochrane and his brother the colonel are on board the flagship,' Mapleton said. 'I'm keeping my weather eye lifting for the gig's return. Come up on the quarterdeck.'

Stella trotted happily at their heels as they paced up and down. There was as yet no sign of the gig. The frigate lay with her head to seaward pointing into the fresh westerly wind, and astern, plainly visible beyond the Isle d'Aix, the ranked hulls and masts of the anchored French fleet showed against the hazy coast of the inner bay. *Impérieuse* was lying less than two miles from the island.

'We've been in twice.' Mapleton nodded towards the enemy. 'Abreast of the Isle d'Aix. Fired one of our eighteen-pounders at 'em by way of compliment. They've a mighty big boom right across the entrance.'

'As we all expected.'

'Not the Admiral. Believe it or not, Bissell, there's not a frigate of Lord Gambier's squadron – and he's got six out there – been within a mile of the Isle d'Aix. He didn't know whether there was a boom or not. But now – ' Mapleton interrupted himself to glance sharply at his companion. 'Your flotilla of fireworks – is it ready for instant action?'

'Every vessel.'

'Good. I know the captain wants to do the trick tonight if the Admiral's agreeable. Conditions couldn't be better.'

Bissell sniffed the air. 'The wind'll rise in the next twenty-four hours.'

'And blow too hard for our purpose. The fireship crews

have to pull for a mile, getting back when they've abandoned ship, and if the sea's running too high – but there's the gig yonder, just leaving the flagship.' Mapleton hesitated. 'Mr Bissell, this is between you and me. The captain's in a very strange humour these days. I've served with him these five years, in action and out of it, and I've never known him turn a hair before. This business – but I'll say no more, except that's it's as well to tread carefully with him. By the same token, I think we'll have your little dog below decks when he comes on board. – Mr Marryat!' he added more loudly to a tall midshipman at the corner of the taffrail. 'Conduct Mr Bissell to his cabin, if you please. Starboard alleyway, next to mine.'

Bissell, followed closely by Stella, went below with Marryat and unpacked his sea-chest in the neat hutch provided for him. He found a handy corner for Stella's blanket and she settled herself obediently at his command. When he came on deck again the sideboys and boatswain's mates were aligned in double rank at the rail and the captain was just stepping aboard to the shrilling of the silver calls. After him came Lieutenant-Colonel Cochrane in full regimentals, his red face redder than usual. The frigate captain, his face set like stone, touched his hat to the quarterdeck and made straight for his cabin below it, speaking curtly over his shoulder as he went.

'Mr Mapleton, Mr Bissell, Colonel Cochrane – in my cabin, if you please.'

The three officers followed him in and were bidden with a gesture to sit at the table. Cochrane set his clasped hands before him on the table and sat frowning at them in silence, for so long that at last Mapleton ventured a question.

'Is the attack to take place tonight, sir?'

The captain was slow to come out of his abstraction and it was Basil Cochrane who burst into speech, plainly venting his bottled-up indignation.

'No, Mr Mapleton, it isn't – and only God and your

damned sheep's-head of an Admiral know why! If the Frogs had asked him to give them time to prepare for a fireship attack he could have done no –'

'Colonel Cochrane!'

At his brother's stern interruption Basil subsided and mumbled an apology. Cochrane passed a hand across his brow and then looked directly at Bissell.

'I beg your pardon, Mr Bissell,' he said evenly. 'I should have said earlier that I'm more than pleased to see you. Your report, if you please.'

As he gave it Bissell saw the lines of strain on the captain's face relax and his eyes take on something of their old eager brilliance. His voice gathered strength and enthusiasm as he spoke.

'You've done well, Mr Bissell – very well. The Admiral has decided not to attack tonight –'

'Wants to pray for the Lord's blessing on it first,' muttered Basil.

' – But I don't doubt we'll have his permission tomorrow,' Cochrane continued unheeding. 'All our dispositions will be made in readiness for that. In a moment I'll acquaint you with my plan in detail. But first – ' he hesitated, biting his lip. 'I think you should be aware of my situation – of our situation relative to Lord Gambier's fleet.'

'Situation of a gang of thieves caught stealing,' Basil growled.

Cochrane frowned at him. 'Spare your interruptions, I beg. All the same, gentlemen, my brother's analogy is not totally inept. I'm looked upon by Lord Gambier's officers as having come here to filch from them the honour – which should have been theirs – of leading the fireship attack.'

'But that's damned nonsense!' Bissell exclaimed involuntarily.

'You mean, sir, they've said this to your face?' demanded Mapleton in the same breath.

The frigate captain hesitated, his eyes hidden beneath

bent brows. When he looked up it was to glance swiftly round the three men and then down at his clasped fingers.

'When Mr Bissell's convoy was sighted,' he said without expression, 'I went at once on board the flagship to request the Admiral's permission for an attack tonight. Rear-Admiral Harvey, of the *Tonnant*, was already on board. Admiral Harvey presented Lord Gambier with a list of officers who, he said, were prepared to lead the attack in my place. I was on the quarterdeck with the flag captain, Sir Harry Neale, and was forced to witness what followed.'

'Half the ship's company heard it,' Basil put in. 'Harvey's got a voice like a foghorn and he was in a damned bad temper.'

'Lord Gambier told him I'd been sent out by Admiralty,' Cochrane went on in the same level tone, 'and Harvey said he didn't give twopence for that. He said the whole fleet had been passed over to favour a jumped-up junior captain and if I was appointed he'd haul down his flag and resign his commission. Lord Gambier said he would be sorry to see an admiral take such measures, whereupon Admiral Harvey broke into a storm of abuse. He told Lord Gambier he'd never seen a man more unfit to command a fleet –'

'Good God!' Mapleton ejaculated.

' – and then stormed off the quarterdeck and into his boat.'

'Not before he'd called Gambier a bumble-headed Bible-thumper,' said Basil, 'which in my opinion is damned sound judgement.'

Cochrane smote the table with his hand and sat up straight in his chair, an expression of disgust on his face.

'Enough of this,' he said sharply. 'You see, gentlemen, why I'm doubly resolved that this attack shall succeed. I'll add this. I've had nothing but courtesy from Lord Gambier himself. He has nominated crews for the fireships and I shall give them their instructions on board *Caledonia* immediately permission to attack is signalled. Now. Here is our plan.'

He outlined it rapidly and concisely. Three of Lord Gambier's frigates – *Aigle*, *Unicorn*, and *Pallas* – would come in and anchor clear of *Impérieuse* and some distance astern, each with a flotilla of fireships in charge. The explosion-vessel, brought alongside *Impérieuse*, would be the first to set off for the boom, and the explosion – which should accomplish the breaking of the boom – would be the signal for the fireships to cast off and follow. The junior officers commanding the fireships would have orders to pass the boom before igniting their fuses and abandoning ship. With both wind and tide to aid them, there was little doubt that the blazing vessels would cover the half-mile of water that would then separate them from the French ships.

'And now for our own floating bomb, Mr Bissell. A converted store-ship, you said?'

'Yes, sir. Masts cut down for courses only.'

'She shall be named the *Courser*, then, during her short spell in service.'

Cochrane was smiling as he rose to fetch a chart from the bulkhead shelf and spread it on the table. The past and its ominous jealousies were behind him and he planned the future as if it was to be a picnic.

'I reconnoitred the boom immediately I arrived. It's across the strait here – from the inner end of the Isle d'Aix to the inner end of the shoal. The seaward end of the island juts in a rocky point – here – and that's our mark for lighting the fuses and abandoning ship. Your comments, Mr Bissell, if you please.'

Bissell considered, frowning. 'The distance is short, sir. I don't know – no one at the Arsenal could tell me – what radius of effect the explosion will have.'

'We have to make certain of its effect on the boom, Mr Bissell,' Cochrane returned a trifle stiffly. 'Our own safety is secondary to that.'

'Of course, sir,' said Bissell, grinding his teeth; Cochrane, it seemed to him, was always putting him in the wrong.

'And equally of course,' said his brother with unusual seriousness, 'the Frogs will be ready for you. Old Sheep's-head has given 'em twenty-four hours and they're not damned fools. They'll have guns in those dismantled fortifications on the Isle d'Aix.'

'Very little chance for their guns on a pitch-dark night, sir,' Mapleton pointed out.

'All the same,' said Basil hopefully, 'if you'd stand in a bit, Tom, and let me try a shot or two, we might do some useful damage.'

Cochrane laughed. 'You'll get your chance with the guns, never fear – but not until tomorrow, when Lord Gambier brings in his ships to finish what we've begun. For the present we can do nothing but wait.'

Wait. It was the key-word for the rest of that day and most of the next. Bissell dined in the wardroom and exercised Stella on deck, learning from his various encounters with officers and men that the whole ship's company of *Impérieuse* were devoted to their captain and spoiling for a fight – preferably with the French but failing them with any other ship's company who said a word against Cochrane.

Next morning, a gloomy day of low hurrying clouds and a rising wind, every eye in the frigate was continually turning to the massed hulls of the big ships two miles away to eastward, but no hoped-for signal fluttered from the flagship's yardarm. Cochrane, coming down from a long spell at the masthead, reported that the French ships had struck their upper masts in anticipation of an attack; but if this, or the lack of any communication from the Admiral, perturbed him he showed no sign of it.

Noon passed and still there was no signal from *Caledonia*. At Bissell's request Mapleton made him acquainted with the four seamen (selected from 250 volunteers, said the first lieutenant with justifiable pride) who were to man the explosion-vessel: Farrow, Ball, Appleby, and Milton, captain's coxswain, a tough-looking quartet.

'Strong as horses, those lads,' Mapleton said as they walked aft. 'You'll need those muscles for the pull back against wind and tide. Sea's rising, too. Let's hope – here we go at last, thank God!'

He ran for the quarterdeck, where Cochrane already had his telescope aimed at the hoist of bunting at *Caledonia*'s yardarm.

And now the dark and heaving waters of the Basque Roads became busy with moving craft. Cochrane's gig took him to the flagship, boats toiled to and fro between the ships of the fleet and the fireship convoy, the three frigates acting as fireship bases took up their stations. Out from the huddle of smaller vessels came the explosion-vessel, bucking across the darkening sea under the main courses on her two stumps of masts, to be made fast to the stern of *Impérieuse*. Bissell lost no time in getting aboard her to check that all was well. He took Stella with him and was once again amused at her obvious pleasure in the smell – presumably manifest to her though not to him – of explosives.

Cochrane, who had just returned from *Caledonia*, met them as they regained the frigate's deck. He was smiling and his eyes gleamed in the fading light.

'Seeing that our *Courser*'s saddled and bridled, Mr Bissell?' he said. 'Excellent. We'll have a fine gallop with the sea that's running now.' He glanced down at Stella, who was eyeing him anxiously. 'You don't propose to take the dog, of course.'

'I do so propose, sir.' Bissell's harsh voice hinted defiance. 'Where I go Stella goes.'

Cochrane's smile vanished. 'Nonsense, man!' he said impatiently. 'This is a damned dangerous mission – surely you realise that. We take our lives in our hands. A dog, getting in everyone's way –'

'Was she in the way on Belle Ile four years ago?' snapped Bissell.

The reprimand he had justly earned didn't come.

Cochrane shut his teeth on it with an audible click.

'Bring the bitch and be damned to you, then,' he said angrily. 'I'll take this matter up with you later, Mr Bissell. For the present, I'll thank you to make your preparations.' He turned away. 'We cast off in the explosion-vessel at two bells of the first watch.'

VI

The Fireships – 2

1

In the utter blackness of the windy night the faint glow that rose and fell under *Impérieuse*'s starboard side seemed unnaturally bright. It was the binnacle lamp by the helm of the explosion-vessel, and its shifting radiance showed the moving shadows of the four seamen who had already boarded her. A cluster of dark figures stood by the frigate's rail, where Lieutenant Bissell, with Stella under his arm, prepared to jump down onto the tossing deck below. As he waited for the *Courser* to rise on the next wave Cochrane's voice, low and quick, spoke close beside him.

'Take this, Basil. If I don't come back take it to her. Tell her where it came from.'

Bissell made his jump, a matter of three or four feet, and landed neatly enough though his thoughts were elsewhere. What had passed from Cochrane to his brother, he felt sure, was a miniature framed in red morocco leather; he was the more sure of it because of the lace handkerchief that reposed in his own inner pocket.

He put Stella down out of the way. Cochrane landed on the deck and sprang to the wheel.

'Cast off all! Hands to the sheets!'

The courses, brailed to the yards with split yarn, were freed at a jerk and the canvas flapped wildly before the sheets were hauled in and belayed. *Courser* heeled steeply as she swung away broadside-on to the waves and then regained an even keel, rising and falling sluggishly with the wind over her stern. The dimly-seen loom of the frigate's hull vanished into the darkness, a darkness so intense that the cockboat towing astern was invisible. No glint of white showed on the crests of the marching waves that hoisted the explosion-vessel onwards, for both wind and tide were driving with her and the waves, though high, were unbroken. The dual thrust on her stern, Bissell reflected, made it no easy matter to hold the course – south-east by south – which was essential to their purpose; Cochrane, he perceived, had called Milton to help him at the wheel.

Somewhere to starboard was the long shoal defending Oléron, and somewhere ahead on the port side was the Isle d'Aix with the rocky headland that was all-important as a distance marker. With that headland (it was no more than a low spit) dead abeam, he and Cochrane had calculated, the boom would be eight cable-lengths ahead. In this universal blackness the compass-dial alone could be their guide for the course, which must take them near enough to the island for that rocky spit to be identified.

But pitch-darkness and a high sea, though they increased the hazards of pilotage, at least nullified the risk of being fired on by the battery on the Isle d'Aix. Even with better visibility the risks of a hit were small, as Mapleton had said; but a single hit from a 32-pounder would be enough to finish them. Bissell thought of the potential volcano a few inches below his feet and ready to erupt: fifteen hundred barrels of powder, three hundred shells, a thousand grenades, a hundred Congreve rockets – if that went up before its due time there wouldn't be a fragment left of the six men on board.

Heavily laden as she was, with only the two low sails on her stumps of masts, *Courser* was lumbering slowly over the waves despite the strong wind. He knelt on the deck abaft the rise of the after-hatch, Stella sniffing excitedly at his elbow, and felt for the two fuses. They protruded through holes drilled in the planking and were protected by a neat shelter constructed to his own design, with the fuse-ends supported clear of the deck to make ignition easy and sure. Cochrane was to light them and had the port-fires in the pocket of his tarpaulin coat, but they had first to be cut.

'Farrow, Appleby!' came Cochrane's shout. 'Keep your eyes skinned, port side. Ball, here to the wheel.'

He came to stoop at Bissell's side. Stella, as if aware of her unpopularity with the captain, trotted away.

'We're making five knots, Mr Bissell, at a guess. Hard to say for certain, but you'd better cut now.'

Eight cable-lengths from the spit to the boom, at five knots. Bissell took a little pair of shears from his pocket.

'Seven-minute fuse, sir.' He drew each end of slow-match through his fingers, feeling the small tufts that marked each inch, and snipped them carefully. 'Fuses ready.'

'Seven minutes,' Cochrane repeated slowly. 'I fancy we shall need every second. See that there's no delay with the boat, Mr Bissell, when the time comes.'

'Aye aye, sir.'

Cochrane stood up and went across to the rail where the lookouts stood peering into the darkness. Bissell adjusted his fuses to a nicety and then followed him. The converted transport was flush-decked with a low rail, and the tall black rollers that hissed alongside, just visible now to his night-adjusted eyes, seemed to tower over her when she wallowed down in the troughs. If Cochrane's calculations were wrong, Bissell was thinking, if she drove straight onto the boom; the huge timber-baulks and chains would be solid as a rock with tide and wind straining them; it would be like running full tilt on a reef. *Courser*'s masts would snap like twigs, she would heel over holed and sinking. In the chaos of such a wreck, would they have any chance of lighting the fuses – or of getting away in the boat?

From somewhere right aft came the sound of Stella's

excited barking. Cochrane had gone to the binnacle and was consulting his watch by its dim light. He sprang back to the rail and spoke tensely.

'Sharp lookout, men. We should be abeam of the island any second now. – Mr Bissell,' he added irritably, 'can't you quiet that damned dog of yours?'

Stella was barking continuously and loudly, the short high-pitched bark with which Bissell had known her to summon his attention to an 18-pounder that had worked its breachings loose. He stumbled aft along the deck and found her on her hind legs in the corner of the rail, her vociferous muzzle pointing over the port quarter. A backstay had been rigged for the mizen and by its aid he swung himself onto the after-rail to stare into the obscurity beyond the wave-tops. A speck of white appeared on the blackness, grew and vanished; appeared and vanished again. He sprang down and ran for'ard with a shout.

'The spit – on the port quarter! We've passed it!'

Cochrane's order came instantly. 'Hands to abandon ship!'

There was no need for more, for every man of the five knew his duty. Bissell's was to ensure that the boat was brought alongside with the utmost speed, and his whole mind concentrated on that. Milton and Ball were lashing the wheel as he dashed past them to the starboard rail, Appleby and Farrow were already hauling on the towrope to bring the boat for'ard. As he cast loose the thick rope for their descent into the boat he saw the flash of flint and steel from the corner of his eye. No brighter flame followed and for a moment he was distracted by the fear that the port-fire would not ignite. Then there came a flare of light that persisted. The fuses were being lit.

'Boat alongside, sir.'

'Over with you, quick.'

The two seamen slid down the rope – it was a couple of fathoms, no more – and Milton and Ball came running to do likewise. Turning, Bissell saw the spluttering port-fire flung overboard and swung himself over the rail, landing awkwardly because the tossing boat chanced to be in a trough. Cochrane came down almost on top of him and they scrambled into the sternsheets as the men at the oars pulled their first stroke.

'Pull short.' Cochrane put the tiller hard over. 'Now – put your backs into it, and give it all you've got.'

The boat, rolling giddily in the black hollow of a wave, had swung round as she rose on the crest and now headed straight back on the course they had come, plunging and soaring into the wind's eye across the dark furrows. Astern of her the *Courser*, left to sail herself, lumbered onwards towards the boom.

'Seven minutes,' said Cochrane. 'I fancy, Mr Bissell, we shall – why, what is it, man?'

Bissell had let out a strange inarticulate roar, between a shout and a groan.

'The dog – left behind.' He swallowed hard. 'Never mind.'

'By God, I'll not leave her!' Cochrane pushed the tiller over. ''Vast pulling starboard, pull port – now together, and lay into it!'

Back sped the boat, with sea and wind to aid her now. Out of the dark grew the shape of the explosion-vessel and a dozen lusty strokes brought them below her quarter. The rope still hung down her side, and scarcely had Farrow, in the bows, grasped it when Cochrane was climbing hand-over-hand with feet braced against the timbers. He vanished over the rail above but reappeared almost at once.

'Bissell – catch!'

Bissell was standing ready in the heaving boat. He grasped and held the little hairy bundle that was tossed down to him and was glad of the darkness to hide the tears that stung his eyes. There was no time for thanks or comment. Cochrane landed on the bottom-boards with a thump and the boat was away again without waiting for his order, swirling round and swooping bows-on to the waves. Bissell put Stella under the stern-thwart. Cochrane, beside him at the tiller, spoke in a loud and cheerful voice.

'Well done, men. Now – pull for your lives.'

The seamen needed no urging. The short powerful strokes of the four oars forced the boat on in the teeth of the wind and the charging seas. But against that opposition her headway was necessarily slow, and Bissell's teeth were clenched hard as he tried to fight down his anxiety. How long had the rescue of Stella taken? It had seemed to occupy a phenomenally short time but it must have been three minutes at the very least. Four minutes to go. How near to the boom had the explosion-vessel been when they left her the second time? What radius had the circle of danger surrounding the coming explosion? Nothing was certain except that the lives of all of them hung by a thread.

The five men with him realised that too. No one spoke. The grunts of the labouring oarsmen and the creak of the oars, the hissing of the wind and the hollow surge of the waves, were the only sounds. Surely four minutes had gone by? A new anxiety gripped Bissell's mind. Suppose his fuses had sputtered out before the spark reached the powder! But no; that would be hardly possible after the tests he had made. Why didn't it come, then? Why –

It came, and with a threefold impact.

Suddenly the boat and its occupants, the rolling seas, the low clouds scudding overhead, were lit by a tremendous blaze of light. It was like a vast cupola filled with orange-red flame and criss-crossed by a myriad glittering streaks – the rocket trails. Shells, grenades, and black unidentifiable objects shot skyward, reaching far out over the boat. Then came the ear-splitting crash of the explosion, stunning the senses so that none of them could say afterwards how long it was before the great wave reached them.

It seemed an upheaval from beneath rather than a

travelling wave. The boat was upflung, tossed aloft on a huge mound of water, and then dropped into a vast trough so deep that its walls of water shut out the glare. The boat swooped and swayed in a flurry of spray, tilting until she seemed certain to capsize, while the men in her clung to thwarts and gunwale. The sudden cessation of chaotic movement, the resumption of a normal rise and fall on normal waves, brought a relief that was shortlived. Something struck the gunwale by Bissell's elbow a glancing blow, and a heavier object fell into the water alongside with a mighty splash – if that had fallen in the boat it would have been the end of them.

'Look yonder!' Cochrane was gripping his arm.

Less than a cable-length from them the sea was seething with white splashes, redly lit by the dying flames. Bissell, his dazed senses recovering slowly, realised that the splashes marked the perimeter of the shower of falling fragments, most of which had passed beyond the boat.

'If we hadn't turned back,' Cochrane muttered, 'we'd have been under that, Bissell.' He raised his voice. 'Lost your oars, men?'

'No, sir!' Milton's tone hinted that respectable seamen didn't lose oars.

'Give way, then.'

Nothing more had fallen near the boat, and now complete darkness had descended again. It was broken, Bissell saw as the boat began to forge through the waves, by poinpoints of yellow light ahead – the guiding-lights on *Impérieuse* and the three frigates. The purpose of their expedition, driven from his mind by the events of the past few minutes, returned with something of a shock. The boom – had the explosion broken it? Cochrane, who had stood up to look astern, answered the unspoken question.

'Nothing to be seen, naturally,' he said, sitting down. 'We'll know in a few minutes. Where the devil are the fireships?'

The boat ploughed on, bucking over the waves. Seawater swilled back and forth over the bottom-boards, and Bissell, lifting a wet and shivering Stella onto the thwart beside him, found a tin baler under the thwart and began to bale.

'The damned fool!' Cochrane exclaimed suddenly.

The first fireship had burst into flame and was driving past half-a-mile away to starboard. She had been ignited far too soon – before coming within half-a-mile of the boom. Another rose of flame broke out, and another, both hopelessly short of their appointed position.

Cochrane thrust the tiller into Bissell's hand and stood up again, balancing in the sternsheets. Across the tossing seas flame after flame blazed up, some few astern of the boat but most abeam of her, driving on divergent courses. One, a brig with her sails already on fire, fled across their bows to end up a few minutes later as a smouldering wreck on the Oléron shoals. Another, which must have been abandoned almost as soon as she left the parent frigate, carried her pyramid of fire so close to *Impérieuse* – now less than a mile ahead – that those in the boat could see the red light reflected on her row of gunports. Away on the starboard quarter three fireships, in line abreast and as correctly spaced as though they were manned, sailed like floating torches directly for the rocks of the Isle d'Aix.

Cochrane had watched the insensate ruin of his plan without speaking a word after that first exclamation. Bissell's initial incredulity had quickly become anger, and the implications of failure raised his temper to boiling-point. That a score of cowardly louts should bring all their efforts to naught! That Cochrane's ingenuity and courage should be discounted, his orders ignored, by a set of malicious, envious junior officers not one of whom was worthy to lick his boots! Unable to contain his wrath, he burst into a storm of curses. A hand dropped on his shoulder, checking him.

'Your commination's a trifle too general, Mr Bissell,' said

Cochrane quietly. 'Four officers at least did their duty, or something near it. Four fireships are well into Aix Roads. Your explosion-vessel broke the boom.'

Bissell could feel no exultation. 'Four – out of twenty? Can they do any damage?'

Cochrane sat down beside him and took the tiller. 'I doubt it. They were ignited before they reached the boom.' He spoke for the four seamen to hear. 'We've done our whole duty. Ten minutes more and it's a tot of rum and dry slops for all of us. And there's one among us,' he added, 'who won't get those though she deserves more. I fancy she'll prefer this to rum.'

He had taken a piece of ship's biscuit from his pocket and was proffering it to Stella, who accepted it with her usual delicacy and crunched it happily. Bissell opened his mouth, hesitated, and plunged into speech.

'As to Stella, sir, I'd like to say – I don't know how to thank you –'

'By stowing your gab,' Cochrane put in quickly, 'if you'll pardon a lower-deck expression. By God, Bissell, but for Stella we might have made as foul a run of it as the fireships have done. How could I leave her?'

Bissell made no answer. He was thinking that of the 537 captains on the Post List only one would have gone back for Stella. The rest, not without reason, would condemn Cochrane for risking the lives of his men. He decided that on this subject he had better 'stow his gab'.

The light in the frigate's rigging gleamed in reflection on the black ridges of the waves as they drew nearer. Beyond the wave-tops, scattered to port and starboard, winked the dying red flames of fireships, stranded and futile on shoal and rock.

*

2

The grey light of six o'clock in the morning of 12th April found *Impérieuse* alone at her station off the Boyart shoal, riding uneasily to her anchor. Wind and sea had both fallen in the night and below the lightening clouds the French coast and its protecting islands lay dark and clear across the furrowed water. The explosion-vessel had made her successful assault on the boom before half-flood of the tide, and now the ebb was setting against the wind and tending to swing the frigate across the tide. These things Lieutenant Bissell took in instantly and automatically as he came on deck with Stella. At the same time he was aware of an atmosphere of excitement and jubilation.

The parties of seamen busy with the morning routine of swabbing and scouring the deck plied their mops with unusual liveliness and chatted animatedly in undertones, while the petty officers and boatswain's mates in charge of them stood in groups talking and gesticulating. Most of the frigate's officers, he could see, were already on the quarterdeck. Four bells were struck as he went up the ladder, to be met by Lieutenant Mapleton with hand outstretched and a beaming smile.

'Felicitations, Mr Bissell – you've done the trick and no mistake!' cried Mapleton, pumping his hand up and down.

His round boyish face was flushed with enthusiasm. Beyond him Haswell and two midshipmen grinned and nodded. Bissell shook his head.

'I don't know what you mean,' he said.

'We've got 'em, sir – we've *got* 'em!' Mapleton held out his open hand and clenched it. 'Like that. Captain hailed from the masthead a moment ago –'

He broke off. Cochrane had sprung down from the mizen shrouds and was bounding up the ladder to the quarterdeck, calling for the signal midshipman as he came.

Midshipman Marryat jumped forward with his pad and pencil.

'Mr Marryat, make this to the flagship, if you please. Ready? 'All the enemy's ships except two are aground.' Sharp as you can.'

'Aye aye, sir.'

Bissell had closed his mouth on a gasp of incredulity. He spoke with an undertone of disbelief.

'Eight of Allemand's ships aground? Eight of the line?'

Cochrane turned towards him. The frigate captain's lean unshaven face was smiling and his eyes were very bright.

'Yes, Mr Bissell – hard aground. Cut their cables at sight of the fireships and there they are, stuck fast on the ebb. Two of them – but aloft with you and see for yourself. It's a sight for sore eyes like yours and mine.'

Bissell thrust his telescope into his pocket, told Stella to stay, and ran to the mizen shrouds. Mr Marryat's hoist of bunting rose with him as he climbed and then fluttered out on its halyard below him as he gained the crosstrees. Far out on the western horizon bulked the close-ranked shapes of Lord Gambier's fleet. He settled himself, turned the powerful glass south-eastward, and focussed it on the French fleet.

They sprang into vision, a disorderly huddle of massive hulls close against the dark line of the shore. Three of them looked like wrecks, for they were lying over so far that their masts were hardly visible and their bilges displayed. The other five grounded ships were lying at all angles and listed heavily. Not one of the eight could bring a gun to bear on an attacking vessel coming in past the Isle d'Aix, and the entrance was clear – not a spar of the boom could be seen. The two big ships that were still afloat must also have cut their cables, he thought, for they were distant at the inner end of the Roads. All Lord Gambier had to do was to send in four 74's on the first of the flood and Allemand's fleet was at his mercy.

Bissell's surge of triumph and elation was mingled with relief; and this relief, he was surprised to find, was on Cochrane's account. Odd that he should be as much concerned that Cochrane should be vindicated as that the French fleet should be destroyed. But the passing thought was lost in the realisation that his own long-held theories had been vindicated beyond expectation. Without the loss of a single British seaman, the fireships had done what a ship-to-ship battle could only have done at tremendous cost. More, indeed. For Allemand's ships were undamaged by shot, and the French admiral had now the alternatives of total capitulation or total destruction.

With a grim smile of satisfaction he turned the glass on the nearer objective of the Isle d'Aix, well under two miles away. Smoke drifted from the chimney of one of the low buildings visible above the shore, showing that there were men there to man the battery. A couple of broadsides from Gambier's ships when they went in would put that battery out of action. It was a moral certainty that 'the greatest victory since Trafalgar' was already won.

When he stepped down on the deck, to be greeted by a relieved Stella, he came face-to-face with Basil Cochrane. The lieutenant-colonel of Foot had wrapped himself in a boat-cloak against the chilly morning wind and his round bewhiskered face was topped by a woollen nightcap.

'You did it after all, by God!' he cried, grasping Bissell's hand. 'Tom's told me the good news. But what the devil is old Sheep's-head doing out there, ten miles from the enemy? He ought to be up and at 'em, damme!'

'The Admiral will make sail on Captain Lord Cochrane's signal, sir,' Bissell answered a trifle stiffly as they crossed the deck; criticism from the junior Service was unwelcome.

'Think so? All he's done so far is hoist an answering pendant.'

Bissell sent Stella to lie down in her corner by the rail and they mounted to the quarterdeck, where Mapleton and

Haswell, with Rigg the third lieutenant and Hoare, lieutenant of marines, stood in a group by the taffrail. The captain was at the after-rail, his telescope levelled at the distant fleet whose upper works were barely visible above the dark sea-horizon.

'Half-an-hour to slack water,' Haswell was saying. 'They're cutting it fine.'

'Too damned fine,' muttered the first lieutenant. 'It'll take 'em an hour to reach our station here –'

Cochrane's voice interrupted him. 'Mr Marryat, make this to the flagship. "Only two afloat".'

'Spelling it out for old Sheep's-head,' commented Basil in an undertone.

The hoist sailed up to the yardarm and the gaze of all the quarterdeck fixed itself on the fleet.

'Flagship acknowledges, sir,' said the signal midshipman, lowering his telescope.

Bissell remembered the glass in his pocket and used it, watching the bristling line of masts on the horizon for any sign of movement. There was none, though he maintained his watch until his eyes watered. The officers at the taffrail muttered among themselves, Cochrane stood motionless with his back to them. *Impérieuse* swung slowly to her anchor-cable, bringing her bows to the wind as the ebb-tide ceased to run. Mapleton spoke suddenly below his breath, as if the words were forced from him.

'God in heaven! Doesn't he understand his chance is going?'

Cochrane could not have heard him but his next order came within a minute.

'Mr Marryat, make "The enemy can be destroyed".'

There was a long pause. The quarterdeck was silent now.

'Flagship acknowledges, sir.'

Five minutes passed and still there was no movement from the fleet. Cochrane snapped his telescope shut and crossed the quarterdeck to the group at the taffrail. His face was set and expressionless and he spoke with unusual abruptness.

'You've duties, gentlemen, I believe. Mr Hoare, you'll exercise your men at stations. Mr Haswell, find the gunner and make an inspection of every gun, tackles and breachings. Take Colonel Cochrane with you. Mr Mapleton, have the masthead lookout relieved and send the hands to breakfast. Mr Bissell,' he added as the quarterdeck cleared, 'we'll walk, if you please.'

They took two or three turns without speaking. The morning had lightened but the sky was still overcast, with a fresh onshore wind wrinkling the waves that hurried towards the French coast. Bissell experienced an overwhelming feeling of sympathy for the man walking beside him, the man whose enterprise and leadership had opened the way for a victory which, as every minute passed, became less and less likely to be achieved. There was nothing Cochrane could do. He had delivered the French fleet into Lord Gambier's hand and there his control of events ended. If the Admiral, for some unimaginable reason, chose to open his hand and let the French escape –

'You saw the ships aground in the Roads,' Cochrane said suddenly. 'Did it seem to you that any of them had suffered damage by fire?'

'No, sir. Not one, so far as I could see.'

' I thought the same. The four fireships that got past the broken boom were heading too far to the west when I saw them. They didn't get near a French ship.'

'All their line-of-battles cut cables at sight of them?'

'Just that. The show of violence, when it comes by fire, is enough. It's what we've said, you and I, all these years, Bissell. Consider the effect of attacks like this on every French harbour and anchorage – every one of them vulnerable, mark you, by reason of the prevailing wind. Landings, too, to draw Bonaparte's troops to the coast north, west and south. A plan could be drawn up –'

He continued to talk, cogently and well, but Bissell sensed that half his mind was elsewhere. Each time they turned to walk for'ard, he noticed, Cochrane's gaze fixed itself on the horizon where the fleet lay immobile and stayed there until they turned again to walk aft. He must be praying to all his gods, thought Bissell, that Gambier would weigh and come in before it was too late. Along the frigate's side the waves, to his seaman's ear, told plainly that the tide was making. In Aix Roads the water would begin its slow rise, would lift those helpless hulls to an even keel, would float them at last and turn them again into fighting ships able to bring their broadsides to bear on any attacker – and the whole operation of fireships and explosion-vessel would have been wasted. The mismanagement of the fireships had been bad enough, but this second piece of bungling was intolerable. He burst into uncontrollable speech, interrupting his companion in mid-sentence.

'God damn it all, he must be mad! If he's not, this delay's pure bloody spite, and a court-martial matter if ever there –'

'Mr Bissell!' Cochrane halted as he spoke, and Bissell perforce halted also. 'I'll have no criticism of senior officers on my quarterdeck.'

'I beg your pardon, sir. I'm damned if I'll beg his. Why, if the Admiral doesn't wish to hazard his seventy-fours,' Bissell went on forcibly, 'there's his six frigates – they alone could finish off the French if they went in now!'

The captain's frown gave place to a faint smile.

'So they could, by God! And I'll tell him so though he breaks me for it.'

He snapped an order at the signal midshipman and a few moments later the hoist was fluttering aloft: *The frigates alone can destroy the enemy*. It almost amounted to a taunt, thought Bissell; and not only the flagship but every other vessel in the fleet would be reading that signal. Surely, for very shame, Gambier must take action.

'Flagship acknowledges, sir,' said Marryat.

Mapleton had returned to the quarterdeck and all three officers stood silent and watchful, their telescopes directed at the distant flagship; the Admiral's signal to weigh must precede a movement of the fleet. They watched in vain. No hoist of bunting rose at *Caledonia*'s yardarm, no canvas showed on that forest of spars. Cochrane turned from the rail.

'You gentlemen haven't breakfasted, I fancy,' he said a little wearily.

'Nor have you, sir,' Mapleton returned. 'And as I have the forenoon watch –'

'I shall stay on deck, Mr Mapleton. Send up some coffee for me, if you please.'

The time was now half-past eight. For the next hour Bissell, for one, was aware of a slowly-rising tide of angry discontent in *Impérieuse* matching the sea-tide that was making into the Aix Roads. The lower deck was as fully aware as the wardroom of what was going on. Milton and his mates had spread the tale of the happenings on the explosion-vessel; Stella's part in the operation had lost nothing in the telling and she was the heroine of the mess-decks. Two hundred and fifty men knew that their captain's daring venture was being treated as of no account by the Admiral and their oaths and grumblings hummed in the 'tween-decks. The mounting tension was broken when, at half-past nine, the masthead lookout hailed the deck to report that Allemand's boats were laying out anchors and rigging cables. Cochrane's signal was at his yardarm within the minute: *The enemy is preparing to heave off.* The knowledge that this was their Admiral's last chance of achieving the looked-for victory held the frigate's decks silent as men and officers waited for him to respond.

And now, it seemed – at the eleventh hour – Lord Gambier was ready to act. The answering pendant had hardly been lowered when a hoist of half-a-dozen flags fluttered from *Caledonia*'s yardarm and with commendable promptitude his fleet made sail. Under main and topsails, in two lines with the flagship leading, the big ships left their station on the horizon and moved slowly inshore. On they came, a splendid sight, with the attendant frigates sailing three on either hand. They were still three miles distant when, at the flagship's signal, they came to the wind, let go their anchors, and took in sail.

Bissell, watching from the quarterdeck with the rest (Stella, on lead, sitting patiently beside him) could scarcely believe his eyes. He was in fullest sympathy with the uproar of groans and oaths that burst from the seamen crowded on the foredeck and Colonel Cochrane's torrent of expletives expressed his own feelings perfectly. The frigate captain's voice rang loud and angry above this tumult.

'Mr Mapleton! What are these idlers doing on deck? I want only the duty watch on deck – and I'll have this quarterdeck clear, gentlemen! The officer of the watch, the signal midshipman, and Mr Bissell will remain.'

While a redfaced Mapleton bellowed orders and the quarterdeck emptied, Cochrane stood at the rail like a figure carved from stone, gazing across the water at the flagship. Bissell could guess at the rage and frustration seething in him as the minutes fled past and Gambier's ships made themselves snug at their new anchorage. Would Cochrane try another signal to the flagship, he wondered? After the signals that had already passed, though, that would be futile. No sign came from the Admiral; no hoist headed by *Impérieuse*'s number rose to tell Cochrane of his intentions, no boat came skimming across the three-mile interval of dark water. The pull of the making tide could be felt on the frigate's hull. Mapleton had come to stand beside Bissell at the taffrail.

'If Lord Gambier's waiting for high water before he goes in,' he muttered, 'our cake's dough. Allemand will warp his ships into the mouth of the Charente. That immobilises them, of course, but they'll be covered by the shore batteries.'

Bissell swung round to face him. 'By God, it's – it's

criminal! When they know about this in England –'

He broke off. His quick movement had slipped Stella's lead from his hand and she had trotted off towards the motionless figure at the rail, the lead trailing behind her. As if she detected a need for sympathy here, she pushed her muzzle against the captain's legs and looked up at him, wagging her tail. Bissell, half-expecting Cochrane in his present mood to turn and kick her, dashed forward to grab the lead. But Cochrane was bending down to stroke her.

'I beg your pardon, sir,' Bissell said hurriedly. 'She – she dragged her cable.'

'Yes,' said Cochrane without looking up. 'Yes!' he repeated, straightening himself suddenly; his eyes flashed and he was smiling. 'Mr Mapleton!'

'Sir!'

'The tide's running fast and the wind's rising. You agree?'

'Well – oh yes, sir.'

'And we've poorish holding-ground here, I fancy?'

Mapleton gaped at him. 'I wouldn't say that, sir –'

'Bad holding-ground,' Cochrane said firmly. 'Hands to man the capstan, Mr Mapleton. Two hands to the wheel. I'll have the anchor hove.'

'Aye aye, sir. But – you'll want sail on her?'

'No, Mr Mapleton. Pay attention. You'll heave-in until the cable's up-and-down, then heave another fathom to clear the bottom. You understand?'

'But she'll drift stern-first – ' Mapleton's puzzled face was suddenly one enormous grin. 'Aye-*aye*, sir!'

He turned and ran to the taffrail shouting orders.

Five minutes later *Impérieuse* began to move under the combined forces of wind and tide. Her yards were bare of canvas, and to a watcher three miles away it would appear that she had lost her holding-ground and was dragging her anchor. Slowly, almost imperceptibly, she glided stern-first towards the Isle d'Aix and the enemy.

3

It was two bells of the afternoon watch when the drifting frigate came within range of the battery on the Isle d'Aix. Not without difficulty (for using the helm in making sternway is a delicate business) she had contrived to keep well over towards the Oléron shore on the west side of the two-mile-wide entrance, and the first shot from the 32-pounders on the island to eastward fell a quarter-mile short. It was now that Cochrane made the signal which he hoped would at last stir his commanding officer to action: *I am in need of assistance.* The code pendants for this were the same as those for *I am in distress*, and when the signal midshipman called his attention to it he remarked with a grin that his lordship would soon see that he was not at all distressed.

While *Impérieuse* held on her stern-first course the white puffs and flat reports from the Aix battery continued, the gunners firing as fast as they could load. But by this time the faster tide in the narrows was bearing her along at increased speed, and the splashes that marked the fall of shot were out of line as well as comfortably short of their mark. She drifted unscathed past the southern tip of the island and came into the wide anchorage of the Aix Roads where – on every hand, as it seemed – loomed the disordered hulls and towering spars of enemy ships.

The anchor had been brought a-cockbill and catted as she passed the Isle d'Aix and now Cochrane's orders rang out loud and fast. *Impérieuse* was transformed with astonishing rapidity from a drifting hulk into a fighting ship. The stirring *rafale* of the marines' drum beating to quarters was followed by a hollow thunder as the frigate's 18-pounders were run out; lines of scarlet-and-white appeared on quarterdeck and foredeck where Hoare's three dozen marines were taking station; courses and topsails flapped and tautened on her yards and she turned across the wind, once more under control.

'Take her below, Mr Bissell – I'll not have Stella hurt.'

Cochrane found time for that between two rapid orders to the helmsman. Bissell obeyed, bundling the reluctant Stella into his cabin, and before he could return on deck three heavy explosions told that some French ship whose guns would bear had opened fire on the impudent British intruder. Cochrane had told him that the quarterdeck would be his station in action and he raced back up the ladder, hearing the roar of *Impérieuse*'s cable running out through the hawse-hole as he went. Cochrane was striding along the deck behind the guns, snapping instructions at the waiting gunners. Up on the quarterdeck Mapleton darted alert glances all round him as the frigate turned slowly to her anchor.

'Five fathoms here,' he shot over his shoulder as Bissell came up. 'And we can fire both broadsides.'

It was a sombre and intimidating scene that met Bissell's gaze. Under a lowering sky and stretching away to the dark rise of the French coast a scant two miles away was a vista of enemy ships, each of them far superior in strength to *Impérieuse*. Half of them were beyond gunshot, a huddle of big hulls close to the land; the tide had lifted them and they had made for the Charente estuary only to strand (according to Mapleton) on the bar at the river-mouth. Nearer, and listing with masts tilted at all angles, were others, frigates and battleships, including the 120-gun *Océan* who was engaged in throwing her guns overboard in an effort to get afloat. Close at hand lay two 74's fast aground, boats busy around them, kedge-anchors out, decks aswarm with men, their rows of gunports unable to bear on the frigate. They were on her starboard hand as she settled to her anchor-cable. On the port hand and a long musket-shot away a slightly smaller vessel was stranded with her flank almost but not quite parallel with the frigate's.

'*Calcutta*, fifty-four,' Mapleton said. 'She's nearly afloat. And there – ' he indicated the 74's – 'are *Aquilon* and *Varsovie*, working like devils to bring guns to bear on us. When they do –'

A triple flash broke from *Calcutta's* side and *Impérieuse* jerked and shuddered to a hit on her hull.

' – we'll catch it hot and strong,' continued Mapleton coolly. 'They mount thirty-two pounders. I fancy those are eighteen-pounders, same as ours, firing on board *Calcutta*, but until she floats she can't give us her whole broadside.'

Cochrane came leaping up the ladder and swung round to shout his orders.

'Port broadside – fire!'

The multiple roar of the 18-pounders split the air and before the clouds of dun smoke rose to hide *Calcutta* Bissell saw the splinters fly from her side and a portion of her after-rail blown into the sea.

'Starboard broadside – fire!'

Down on the deck amidships Colonel Cochrane, conspicuous in red coat and gold braid, waved his hat and his guns fired in near unison at the two close-lying 74's.

'Independent fire!' yelled Cochrane.

And now the thunder of the guns raged unceasing. The billowing clouds of smoke gave only fitful glimpses of the enemy ships and the acrid stink of burnt powder filled Bissell's nostrils. He had been in action often enough before but never without some pressing duty to occupy him, and he found his own inaction in the midst of a battle hard to bear. In addition, the incessant din began to numb his mind, so that he lost all count of time and had to force his senses to note what was going on around him. Cochrane and his first lieutenant were pacing the quarterdeck as if the uproar on every hand was non-existent. At the port rail Captain Hoare of the marines was directing his men as, when the drifting smoke allowed, they tried dropping-shots at *Calcutta*'s deck. Bissell went to stand at the after-rail, and as he reached it the deck below him leapt and shook to two hits in rapid succession. At the same instant the mizen shrouds parted with a twang and swung inboard above the deck. He waited for a clearance of the smoke to give him a sight of *Calcutta*; Cochrane, he knew, had been hoping to disable the more powerful ship before the tide – now almost at its full – lifted her so that she could bear with her whole broadside. A gap blew and he saw her.

The frigate's gunners had hit her again and again and she was half a wreck, her foremast gone and great ragged gaps in her rail. But the Tricolor still fluttered at the main and she was afloat, with her broadside fronting *Impérieuse* and the bright flashes of her 18-pounders jetting from the gunports. He wondered why there were so few of those flashes until he realised that a number of the ports were mere blackened holes.

The curtain of smoke drew across again, the endless detonations of the guns continued. There came a loud crack, sharp enough to be heard through the gunfire. The frigate's foretopmast had been shot through. Some time later – how much later Bissell couldn't tell – *Impérieuse* reeled to a tremendous impact and there was a piercing shriek from for'ard.

'Starboard side,' he heard Cochrane say. 'The seventy-fours have opened on us. See what the damage is, Mr Mapleton.'

Then another sound, a distant augmentation of the nearer gunfire, forced itself on his consciousness and he leaned outboard over the quarter to look whence it came. Dimly through the smoke-wreaths he could see the Isle d'Aix and the entrance to the Roads, and under the darkening afternoon sky the line of big ships and the orange flashes of their guns as they fired on the island battery. Lord Gambier, tardy as ever, was sending assistance. As he turned to report this to the captain Mapleton came up to the quarterdeck, ducking involuntarily as a ball from one of the 74's screeched very close overhead.

'Number four gun smashed to blazes,' he said breathlessly. 'Three men killed. And we've a dozen wounded in the sickbay,' he added. 'Some of 'em are like to die, sir.'

Before Cochrane could reply there was a sudden screech of cheering from the deck and peering through the smoke they saw that *Calcutta*'s mizen-mast lay across her deck in a tangle of rigging. As they watched, the Tricolor came slowly down from her one remaining mast.

'Mr Haswell!' Cochrane yelled from the taffrail. 'Port guns cease fire – she's struck!' He spun on his heel. 'Mr Mapleton, for'ard with you and send a boat to take possession. Mr Hoare, your men may stand down.'

Mapleton sprang down the ladder and the marines and their officer followed with less precipitation. Bissell stepped forward.

'Sir, the Admiral has sent in three of the line –'

A blow like the impact of a giant hammer struck the frigate's side close to him and made him stagger. The 32-pounder ball that smashed into *Impérieuse*'s starboard quarter was deflected upwards and tore a great rent in the deck planking, sending the long splinters flying like arrows. Neither Bissell nor the signal midshipman at the angle of the taffrail was hit but Cochrane was flung to the deck. He was struggling to rise as Bissell reached him, and replied tersely to the lieutenant's anxious question.

'A scratch, no more.' He winced and relapsed into a sitting position. 'Continue your report, Mr Bissell. You were saying that Lord Gambier has sent –'

'Three of the line and three frigates. And it's more than a scratch.'

Bissell was kneeling beside the captain with a hand supporting his shoulders. The back of Cochrane's blue coat was torn across for eighteen inches just below the shoulder-blades and the shirt bulging through the gap was drenched with blood.

'I'll get you down to the sickbay,' he said.

'I shall not leave the quarterdeck!' Cochrane snapped. 'A flesh-wound – a strip of plaster will serve. Where was this squadron when you saw it?'

'Coming in past the Isle d'Aix, sir. Raise your left arm a trifle.'

Bissell was removing the captain's coat. Cochrane, with a frown and a wince, did as he was told.

'They'll pass between us and the seventy-fours,' he said. 'Mr Marryat!'

'Sir!'

'My compliments to Colonel Cochrane and he's to cease fire. Then get a roll of plaster from the surgeon.'

'And bring water and a swab!' Bissell shouted after the retreating midshipman.

He tossed the torn coat aside. As he began to draw off the blood-soaked shirt *Impérieuse* shuddered to another hit on her hull.

'Near our waterline, by the sound of it,' Cochrane muttered; and added more sharply, 'God damn it, man, let me stand up!'

The deafening racket of the starboard guns had ceased and in the comparative silence his voice rang strangely loud.

'If you do,' said Bissell, 'you'll regret it, and that's a moral certainty. You're losing a deal of blood. We can do something to check it if you stay sitting.'

The captain's back was an ugly sight. The razor-sharp splinter had slit the flesh to the bone in a cut more than a foot long and blood was pouring from the gaping wound. Bissell made him lean backwards, supporting himself with his arms and arching his back to press the edges of the wound together, and was using the shirt to staunch the bleeding when the thunder of a broadside turned both their heads. Out beyond the frigate's starboard side, seen through the splintered ruin of the rail, moved the big brown hulls of Gambier's 74's.

'It's for them to finish the task,' Cochrane sighed. 'We're out of it. Poor *Impérieuse*!'

Bissell followed the direction of his gaze. Now that the smoke had cleared it was possible to see the extent of the damage suffered by the frigate. Her sails were in shreds, foretopmast and mizen yard dangled shattered in the slings, the severed ends of rigging and shrouds hung in untidy festoons. Along the deck lay the piles of splintered wood from the rail and the smashed boats. She had taken on a list from the hit on her waterline.

'At least she's taken a prize,' he said, impelled to offer comfort however inadequate. 'And no doubt the seventy-fours will take others.'

'A couple, perhaps. Or none, if the French captains set fire to them as I'd do in their –'

Cochrane stopped abruptly. He was looking at the deck where Bissell had dropped his coat. Beside the coat lay a small oblong of red morocco leather, fallen from one of the pockets. Bissell picked it up and laid it on the captain's outstretched thigh.

'Thank you,' Cochrane said absently; he glanced up and met the lieutenant's eye. 'It's the prize denied to us that we can never forget, Bissell.' He hesitated. 'You too, I fancy?'

'Yes,' said Bissell.

Midshipman Marryat clattered up the ladder panting, carrying a leather bucket half-full of water and a roll of plaster. Bissell told him peremptorily to kneel on the deck and lend a hand.

'Aye aye, sir,' said Marryat, finding his breath. 'Mr Mapleton told me to say there's four feet of water in the hold and he's starting the pumps, sir. And the *Varsovie* – the Frenchman, sir – she's abandoned ship and the Frogs have set her on fire, sir.' He paused. 'Most of the French have got off and away inshore, sir.'

'Yes,' Cochrane said heavily. 'Well – I did what I could.'

'There's not a man alive could have done more,' said Bissell; and meant it.

4

Captain Lord Cochrane closed his prayer-book, the boatswain nodded at the two seamen acting as dispatchers. The last of the six bodies, sewn in its hammock, slid from the tilted planks into the grey waters at the edge of the Boyart shoal.

'Carry on, Mr Mapleton, if you please,' said Cochrane.

He put on his hat and climbed stiffly to the quarterdeck; stiffly, because of the twenty-three stitches in his wounded back. At Mapleton's order the burial-party dismissed, and in two minutes the sounds of hammering and sawing which had filled the ship all that day began again, replacing a comparative silence in which the ceaseless *clank-clank-clank* of the pumps had made a background to the captain's reading of the service. Those pumps were gaining fast now, the carpenter's party having made good progress in the plugging of the shot-holes, and there would be no need to rig a fothering-sail as had at first been proposed.

Lieutenant Bissell crossed the deck to where the patient Stella, bidden to 'stay' during the burial-service, awaited her release. A word and a pat of the hand set her free and she scampered off to investigate the nearest working-party. Along the decks and high in the rigging the men were still at work on the fitting and splicing that had occupied them since first light. There was little doubt now that *Impérieuse* would be ready for sea tomorrow; and Bissell knew that her captain hoped for a chance to strike another blow at Allemand's demoralized ships even though most of them were by now safely under the batteries of the Charente estuary.

He shook his head, frowning, foreseeing a desperate attempt doomed to failure. And yet, remembering the First Lord's emphatic words, he could sympathise with Cochrane. *The Admiralty is bent on destroying that fleet.* To leave a task undone, though the responsibility for that was not his, must be gall and wormwood to Cochrane as it would have been to Nelson.

Standing at the rail, he could see the evidence of what had been achieved. Beyond the grey outline of the Isle d'Aix, its battery now smashed and silent, a haze of smoke marked the smouldering remains of four French ships. *Calcutta*, who should have been their prize, had been set on fire when it had been found impossible to free her from the shoal; *Aquilon* and *Varsovie* had been burnt when their crews had abandoned them; another 74, *Tonnerre* had blown up during the previous night. Six ships of the line and four frigates of the French fleet had saved themselves, thanks to Lord Gambier's ineptitude, and it was a moral certainty (in Bissell's opinion) that Admiral Allemand would have taken steps to make them immune from further attack.

The squadron that Gambier had sent in yesterday afternoon had been recalled by signal lights at dawn. Bissell had been on deck when, heading out to sea, they had filed past the frigate anchored in her advanced position, the three frigates in line bringing up the rear. *Indefatigable* had passed within half-a-cable of *Impérieuse* and Cochrane had hailed her to suggest that she might anchor and join in his attempt on the morrow; to which Captain Rodd replied tartly that he was ordered to rejoin the fleet. The last frigate in line, *Pallas*, steered so that she could hail *Impérieuse* herself. *Pallas* had been Cochrane's ship three years ago when he had entered Aix Roads to chart the soundings, and her present captain, George Seymour, knew Cochrane of old. It had done Bissell's heart good to hear that shouted exchange.

'Captain ahoy! D'you want *Pallas* to remain in company, Tom?'

'And welcome, George! That's if you've had no signal to the contrary.'

'Can't read signals before breakfast. I'm with you.'

And *Pallas* had put her helm over and anchored well clear, two cable-lengths nearer the island.

Not for the first time, Bissell realised with some surprise that his pleasure in this token of comradeship was chiefly on Cochrane's account. Six years ago, he remembered, he (like many another) had put Captain Lord Cochrane down as a show-away, a boaster, all dash and glitter; and the discovery that he was Kathy Barnes's hero had of course tended to bolster that opinion. Now he was off on an entirely different course, heart and soul behind Cochrane, with him in all that he did or suffered. It was an odd phenomenon, and he was contemplating it, not with entire satisfaction, when Basil Cochrane came on deck. Stella, with whom Basil was a great favourite, greeted him rapturously and the two of them joined Bissell at the rail.

'This craft's beginning to look like a fighting ship again,' Basil said, looking round him and rubbing his hands. 'She'll be fit for our foray tomorrow, I take it?'

'No doubt of that, Colonel.'

'Good. I look forward to having my guns in action over yonder.'

'We've to get within eighteen-pounder range first,' Bissell reminded him, 'and it's odds the French have tucked themselves away behind two miles of shoals.'

'Well, I hope we can do some damage, for *his* sake.' Basil nodded towards where his brother paced the quarterdeck. 'Old Sheep's-head may count four out of ten ships destroyed as a victory but Tom don't.' He lowered his voice. 'This has hit him damned hard. He counts it a defeat, y'know.'

'So it was,' Bissell rejoined harshly. 'Lord Cochrane was defeated by his own Service. I'm ashamed, sir, that a military officer should have witnessed it.'

The Colonel looked embarrassed. 'Oh, come now, Bissell,' he protested. 'One bloody old fool of an admiral doesn't damn the whole Navy. But by God!' he added. 'Little Stella here could give Gambier points for sense and beat him. – Where is she?'

Stella had been sniffing at the crack of the aftermost gunport. Now she trotted to her master, looked up at him, and gave a short sharp bark.

'And there you are!' Basil was pointing across the water. 'She knew there was a boat making for us. Give her a cocked hat and an inch or two of gold braid and she'd manage our affairs for us.'

Bissell was focussing his telescope on the approaching boat, a cutter under sail. She was halfway between the frigate and the massed hulls of the fleet three miles away, and he could make out the black jerseys of her crew; it was Lord Gambier's habit to clothe his boat-crews in sombre uniform.

'She's from the flagship,' he said.

'Then she won't be bringing good news,' said Basil uneasily.

They watched the cutter speeding towards them, mainsail and job goose-winged to the following breeze. She came neatly alongside and a young lieutenant clambered aboard the frigate, to be formally received by Mapleton and conducted to the quarterdeck where he handed a letter to the captain. Cochrane, it seemed to Bissell, took a long time to read the letter. At length he came down from the quarterdeck, exchanged a brief word with Mapleton (who had hastily summoned two boatswain's mates to pipe him over the side) and climbed slowly and stiffly down into the cutter, which was away close-hauled with exemplary smartness. The first lieutenant dismissed his impromptu side-party and came across to the two officers by the rail. His usually cheerful face wore a worried expression.

'Summoned to report to the Admiral,' he said briefly.

'And you think it might be a wigging?' suggested Basil, frowning.

'I do not, sir. It's an uncommon compliment to a post-captain when an admiral sends his cutter for him. No – I'm concerned lest the captain should speak his mind to Lord Gambier. He feels very strongly that enough has not been done against the French.

'So do we all, by God!' Basil exploded; he picked up Stella and held her out. 'Here's one that's done more against the French this campaign than Admiral Lord Gambier!'

Mapleton cast a hasty glance round him. 'For God's sake keep your voice down, Colonel! Let a lower-deck man hear that and repeat it as his own opinion, and he'd get a flogging or worse.'

'I cry *peccavi*,' muttered the Colonel, setting the dog down.

'It's true enough all the same,' Bissell said. 'And it'll be said by people at home when they learn about this business.'

'Let them say,' Mapleton said shortly. 'They can't be court-martialled and broke for it. The captain can.'

He turned with some abruptness and went up to the quarterdeck.

Bissell took Stella below to have her meal and then had some food himself in the wardroom. The galley fire was out during repairs and there was no regular supper, and his only companion was Haswell, the second lieutenant. Though dusk had fallen the hammering of the carpenter's parties still went on, completing repairs to the shattered rail, and its reverberations prevented them from hearing any other sound except their own raised voices. The first intimation that Cochrane had returned from the flagship came from Midshipman Marryat, who brought the captain's compliments and a request that Mr Bissell would come to his cabin.

Shouted orders brought the noise of hammering to an end as Bissell came on deck. A light glimmered in the captain's day-cabin below the quarterdeck and when he entered Cochrane was sitting at his table below the hanging oil-lamp. His lean face looked pale in the lamplight and he held himself stiffly, leaning slightly forward to keep his wounded back from touching the chair.

'Sit down, Mr Bissell, and let us drop formality,' he said with a faint smile. 'I sent for you partly because I feel the need of a confidant and partly because you and I have been in this affair together since its inception. I feel you should know the present state of affairs.'

'Thank you, sir,' Bissell said.

'I'll cut it short.' Cochrane's voice became flat and devoid of expression. 'The Admiral required my final report so that he could close his dispatches. I begged him to wait until a further attempt had been made against the French and he declined. I reminded him that the First Lord's order to destroy the French fleet, given to me personally, had not been carried out. Lord Gambier replied that enough had been done and that he would risk no further action.'

'Then tomorrow's attack is called off?' Bissell demanded incredulously.

'It is. I pressed his lordship as hard as a junior captain might, Bissell – to no avail. He was adamant. I could do no more without jeopardising my Service career and yours too, since you are associated with me. But mark this.' Cochrane's voice took on a new note. 'As a naval officer I'm debarred from speaking my mind about an admiral's shortcomings but as a member of Parliament I can call them to the attention of the House. Be sure I shall do so.'

'And by God I'll support anything you say!' Bissell said vehemently. 'There was never an affair so mismanaged –'

'No, Bissell. My thanks, but you'll keep clear of this, if you please. The member for Westminster will be deliberately stirring up a wasp's nest and the consequences must fall on him alone.' The captain rose slowly and stiffly to his feet. '*Impérieuse* is ordered to take Sir Harry Neale with the Admiral's dispatches to England. We sail for Portsmouth tomorrow.'

VII

The Prize

1

'GREAT NAVAL VICTORY IN THE AIX ROADS', shouted the *Morning Post*. 'FRENCH FLEET TOTALLY DESTROYED', cried the *Morning Chronicle*. Their younger contemporary *The Times*, usually sober as befitted an organ of Government, nevertheless echoed the words of the First Lord of the Admiralty in Parliament: 'This is the greatest victory since Trafalgar.' Bonfires were lit, songs hastily written in celebration, broadsheets printed and circulated. Government authority and Government agents ensured that the public were made fully aware of the Government's triumph.

Captain Lord Cochrane, in these accounts, was given full credit for his heroic part in the attack. He was awarded the Knighthood of the Bath; a signal honour, for only one other post-captain had ever received a KB and that was John Jervis, now Earl St Vincent. As for Admiral Lord Gambier, he and his fleet were to be the recipients of a vote of thanks proposed by the Leader of the House of Commons. Even Lord Cochrane's most devoted admirers were somewhat dashed, muttering of ingratitude, when it was learned that the frigate captain (as member for Westminster) had told the First Lord that he intended to oppose the vote with all the eloquence at his command.

William Bissell, himself one of those admirers, supported him with a fierce approval. He had heard Cochrane describe the Aix Roads business as 'the most reprehensible failure that ever disgraced the naval service', and he fully agreed with him. Whether jealousy, resentment, or sheer incompetence in the high command had been responsible for that failure, the man who had caused it must be exposed or the Royal Navy's honour would be for ever smirched. To Bissell the covering-up of blatant incompetence, the unjustified claims of a great victory, were crimes which infuriated him the more because he could make no protest that anyone would listen to. Cochrane alone had the power to make known the truth.

The newspaper accounts of the affair had not failed to mention Lieutenant Bissell, who as a result of it had received promotion to the rank of Master and Commander. ('Least they could do,' Rob Knott had muttered when he heard of it.) The *Chronicle* had somehow got hold of the story of Cochrane's return to the explosion-vessel to rescue a dog named Stella; which probably meant that one of the four seaman-volunteers had been talking. This was not precisely fame and fortune, but Bissell was pleased with his promotion, which not only raised him within a single step of the coveted post-captaincy but also nearly doubled his former pay of five pounds twelve shillings a month. On the strength of it he removed from the Cloak Lane lodging which he had occupied when in London to more presentable quarters in Hay's Mews, a short walk from Rob Knott's house in Brook Street.

Rob had indeed invited Bissell to use his house while he was ashore. But Rob had quietly married Mrs Odger his landlady, to regularize (as he put it) his establishment; and though it appeared to be rather a marriage of convenience than a love-match Bissell preferred to leave the newly-weds to themselves and visit Rob now and then. He also indulged himself in a new uniform, with the white trousers that were now being worn by naval officers instead of breeches. And he was wearing this, with the new single epaulette of his rank on the left shoulder of his blue coat, when he stood outside the door of Number Four Bryanstone Square on a fine summer afternoon.

He had been standing there for some little time trying to summon courage to sound the knocker; so long, indeed, that passers-by had eyed him curiously and Stella, washed and brushed and on a new leather lead, had ventured to prod his legs with her nose. Bissell was not at all confident that his morsel of current fame and his step of promotion were enough to warrant his presenting himself again as Kathy's suitor. But for Rob Knott's assertion (based, perhaps, on recent experience) that every woman wanted to be asked at least twice, he might not have got this far.

At last, nerving himself, he reached for the knocker and banged it heartily. After a short interval the door was opened by the same supercilious manservant who had opened it to him on that rainy morning four years ago.

'William Bissell, of His Majesty's Navy, to see Miss Corbett Barnes,' he said, brusquely to hide his nervousness.

Stella emitted a very small growl and the man eyed her with disapproval.

'I will take up your name, sir,' he said shortly, and retired leaving the door slightly ajar.

Bissell waited, his heart beating faster than ususal hurriedly considering the approach he had planned. Stella, with him because she had brought about their first meeting – the interval of years during which her handkerchief had always been close to his heart – was that his best course? Or would it be better to come up by long reaches to port and starboard, first dealing with the pleasant summer weather, then the health of her aunt –

'Miss Corbett Barnes is not at home, sir.'

The manservant was back, looking down his nose at him. Bissell glared incredulously.

'You gave my name correctly? Bissell. B-I-double-S –'

'I gave that name, sir. Miss Corbett Barnes –'

'To the lady herself?'

'To the lady herself, sir. Miss Corbett Barnes is not – at – home.'

The door closed with something approaching a slam.

Bissell stood for a moment without moving. Then he gave his head a shake and drew a long breath. This was final, then. He had been a fool, perhaps, to expect anything else. He turned away.

'Come, Stella,' he said quietly. 'We'll visit Rob.'

Stella gave a single joyous bark and came near to pulling him over as she frisked down the steps.

It was a longish walk from Bryanstone Square to Brook Street, where Rob was expecting him. Bissell stalked along the dusty crowded streets and alleys with little consciousness of the jostling throngs or the clatter of wagon and carriage, his mind a turmoil of disjointed thoughts. He was aware, despite his bitter disappointment, of a burden lifted from him. All that morning he had been unable to rid himself of a feeling of guilt, a half-conviction that in again seeking to propose marriage to Kathy he was stealing an unfair march on Thomas Cochrane. He had told himself, in vain, that this was totally unreasonable, that she had refused Cochrane and Cochrane had accepted that refusal as final; his brother had held that to be so, and Cochrane's own words as he sat wounded on the deck of *Impérieuse* surely confirmed it. 'It's the prize denied to us that we can never forget', he had said, implying that the denial, for him, was final. Well, it was final for William Bissell now.

A tug on the lead recalled his attention to Stella and he stopped while she modestly relieved herself in the gutter. Here was one, he reflected, who was far from displeased by the outcome of this morning's call. Stella, he felt sure, knew what that closed door meant and was glad of it; she had always been jealous of his attachment to Kathy. Her sprightly gait as they walked on had the self-satisfied confidence of an admiral on the deck of his flagship, and he remembered Basil Cochrane's whimsical comment: 'Give her a cocked hat and an inch or two of gold braid and she'd manage our affairs for us'.

They dodged between two wagons in Queen Anne Street and turned into narrower lanes where he could release her from the lead to trot at his heels. There was comfort in her familiar company and when he found his thoughts veering towards Kathy and the end of his hope of her he wrenched them resolutely back to Stella.

It occurred to him now that while a dog could hardly be said, seriously, to manage a man's affairs for him Stella had certainly influenced the course he had steered during the past seven years. But for Stella he would never have met Kathy and fallen in love with her. But for Stella's timely warning he might now be mouldering on the sea-bottom of the Aix Roads, and the rest of the explosion-vessel's crew too. And if Stella hadn't been on board Cochrane would not have gone back for her and Bissell would not have become Cochrane's devoted admirer and friend. There had been that business on Belle Ile, too, and the way she had drawn his attention, in the nick of time, to the rockets aboard *Brunswick* –

But this was too fanciful. The blow he had just received, though he had tried to shrug aside its effect, must have shaken his wits after all. They turned into Brook Street and he knocked on the door of Number Seventeen, which was opened to him by Mrs Knott, late Odger.

If like cleaves to like, Rob Knott and his new wife were well suited. Except that she had, presumably, two legs under her voluminous skirt the lady closely resembled Rob, being short and sturdy with a squarish goodhumoured face and a disinclination to waste words. She welcomed the visitors with a smile and a word and took them to the back parlour which was Rob's sanctum and workroom. Rob, who was working at the plan of some Congreve device, unhooked a crutch and swung himself off his stool at their entrance, his glance going at once to Bissell's face.

'Mrs Knott, my dear,' he said quickly, 'the brandy bottle from the top shelf, if you please, and two glasses.' He reached down to pat Stella as his wife left the room. 'No go, then?' he said without looking up.

'I got no further than the door,' Bissell said. 'She declined to see me.'

'Oh. Take a chair, Will.'

They sat down. Rob, frowning, spoke again after a brief silence.

'You'll try again?'

'No.'

'Ah. There are other fish in the sea, Will.'

'Not for me, Rob.'

'Just a thought,' Knott said.

Mrs Knott brought bottle and glasses and went out, taking Stella with her to give the dog a drink of water. Rob filled a generous measure for his friend and a dram for himself.

'We've never wetted your epaulette,' he said. 'This'll do it.'

They drank. Bissell set down his empty glass and found it possible to smile at his companion.

'Thanks, Rob. I'm dismasted but not a total wreck. We'll leave it at that, if you please.'

'And I've some news for you,' Knott said, plainly glad to change the subject. 'Mr Congreve left here five minutes before you came. He brought me the plan yonder.'

'A new rocket?'

'Aye. With a delaying fuse for the explosive charge – but that's by the way. He'd come from the Admiralty. Saw the First Lord's secretary there. Admiral Lord Gambier's demanded a court-martial on himself for his actions in Aix Roads.'

'By God!' Bissell sat up, his reverse of the morning forgotten. 'It'll be Cochrane's opposition to the vote of thanks that drove him to that – and by God again, Rob, Gambier's scuttled himself!'

'Don't know so much,' Rob muttered.

'Damn it, man, the truth must come out at a court-martial! Cochrane will see to that.'

Knott wagged his head doubtfully. 'Whose truth? Lord Cochrane's or Lord Gambier's? Admiral points out he destroyed four enemy ships of the line without damage to his own. Claims full marks. Captain says admiral was at fault in not risking his ships to destroy more of 'em. Who's right?'

'But there was no risk, Rob!' Bissell retorted forcibly. 'Less than there was for Admiral Byng fifty years ago when he took his ships out of danger at Minorca, anyway. And what had the court-martial to say to Byng? Neglect of duty – disgraced – condemned to death. If Byng deserved that surely Gambier does.'

'Byng's crime was losing Minorca. For that, the mob and the City nabobs were ready to pull Government down. Government chose the obvious scapegoat and shot him to save themselves.' Rob shook a solemn finger at his friend. 'Don't pin any hopes to this court-martial, Will. It's politics, and politics is another name for lies.'

Bissell shrugged his shoulders. 'You're wrong. When's Gambier's court-martial to be held?'

'In ten days' time.'

'They'll summon all the relevant witnesses – they must do. And I'll be one of them. You'll see then, Rob, that Lord Gambier will be made to pay for the plainest neglect of duty that ever was on sea or land.'

Rob, looking troubled, drummed his fingers on the broadcloth that covered his stump and then nodded.

'I hope you're right. We'll have another on it, just one finger.' He poured brandy and raised his glass. 'And a toast, Will – "confound their politics"!'

*

2

In the big dining-room at Palace Yard the clock over the mantelpiece whirred and struck four. William Bissell glanced at it and continued to scowl at his hands clasped before him on the table. Basil Cochrane banged the table with his fist and broke a gloomy silence.

'They're taking long enough, God damn them!' he exploded.

'Lord Cochrane will have a deal to say,' Bissell pointed out, forcing himself to speak hopefully.

'Tom'll say what they let him, and it's Tom's word unsupported. If you and I had been there –'

The Colonel shook his head and fell silent.

The two were awaiting Captain Lord Cochrane's return from the court-martial. Half-a-mile away in the big room at the Admiralty eight admirals and senior captains were sitting in judgement on the actions of Admiral Lord Gambier in the Aix Roads, by Lord Gambier's own request. Despite their application to the First Lord, neither Colonel Cochrane nor Lieutenant Bissell had been allowed to give evidence; because he had asked for a court-martial on himself Lord Gambier was entitled to call only such witnesses as he wished. ('And I'll wager the Board of Admiralty put him up to that!' Basil had exclaimed when he heard of it.) Since Cochrane's objection to the vote of thanks had been the prime reason for the court-martial he had of course to be present as a witness, though Lord Mulgrave had done his best to get rid of him by offering him immediate command of a squadron and freedom to do what he liked with it. Bissell still clung obstinately to the notion that the truth about the Aix Roads fiasco must emerge when there was such a man as Captain Lord Cochrane to tell it. Basil, unusually pessimistic, was of another opinion.

'Every man in the room yonder,' he said now, jerking his

head in the direction of Whitehall, 'bar one, that is, has but one aim. That's to get old Sheep's-head out of it with his reputation enhanced instead of lowered. If they can't do that, with Government shoving hard from behind – well, they'll deserve to be shot, the lot of 'em.'

'And if they succeed?' Bissell muttered.

'No "if" about it. They'll succeed, Bissell. And by inference unlimited blame'll be thrown upon Tom.'

Basil relieved his feelings with an oath and reached for the decanter of wine, half full, which was on the table between them. He lifted it, paused, and set it down again without filling his glass.

'Like enough he'll be in need of all that,' he said sombrely.

As he spoke the clatter of hooves and wheels sounded and stopped outside. A few moments later Cochrane entered the room. He placed his hat and sword on the table and went straight to the window, which he threw open.

'Acquitted,' he said shortly, without turning.

Basil splashed wine into a glass. 'Take a drink, Tom.'

'Thanks, Basil.'

Cochrane came to sit down at the table. He drained the glass at a draught but stayed his brother from refilling it.

'I'll not drown my sorrows,' he said with a faint smile. 'I was hoarse from talking and that's cured it.'

'You spoke, then?' said Bissell. 'You told them –'

'I answered seven questions, Mr Bissell, each question carefully chosen. When I tried to say anything further I was ruled out of order.'

Basil slammed his hand down on the table. 'There you are! That's the damned jiggery-pokery you'd expect.'

'The court was perfectly correct in that matter, Basil. There was other – jiggery-pokery, however.'

The captain's half-smile vanished and his lean face showed signs of the strain he had been subjected to. His voice as he went on speaking was level and unemphatic.

'I put my chart in evidence, the French chart with my own soundings added. We used it, you remember, for our operations. It was disallowed because it was a French chart – thrown under the clerk's table and left there. Two charts prepared by Stokes, *Caledonia*'s sailing-master, were accepted instead.'

'But no one from the fleet had been in the Roads!' Bissell interjected.

'We know that. The court didn't. Stokes's charts showed imaginary shoals narrowing the entrance to half its actual width. When the court saw this it was agreed unanimously that Lord Gambier had displayed a seamanlike prudence in not allowing me to tempt his seventy-fours into Aix Roads.'

'God damn it all!' Basil shouted. 'he did send three seventy-fours into Aix Roads – when he was forced to!'

Cochrane nodded. 'Just so. I contrived to convey that much information to the court. It was agreed – again unanimously – that this proved beyond any shadow of doubt that the Admiral had pressed his attack to the very limits of the possible.' He shrugged his shoulders. 'He was acquitted. And, one may say, with acclamation.'

The Colonel, restraining an outburst with evident difficulty, eyed his brother anxiously.

'And you, Tom?' he demanded. 'What had this damned farce of a court to say to you?'

'Not one word. What use were words once the verdict was pronounced? I rose from my place, bowed to the court, and retired with what dignity I could muster. But before I left the Admiralty I called on the First Lord's secretary.' Cochrane looked at Bissell. 'An old shipmate of yours, I believe.'

'Peter Windham, *Orion* seventy-four,' Bissell said.

'Mr Windham kindly divulged some news of our futures. You're shortly to be given a command, Mr Bissell, a sloop. For myself – ' Cochrane paused. 'I'm superseded as captain of *Impérieuse* and it's unlikely that I shall ever be employed again.'

'Now by all the devils in hell!' Basil's round face was flushed with anger. 'If ever there was rank injustice –'

'That'll do, if you please.' Cochrane stood up, a little wearily. 'You'll both excuse me, I know. I've much to think about.' He went towards the door, halted halfway, and came back. 'I think we may not meet again, Bissell.'

He held out his hand. Bissell gripped it in silence. Cochrane went out and the door closed behind him.

It was plain from Basil Cochrane's expression as he swung round to face the lieutenant that he was about to embark on a long execration of the court-martial and everyone concerned in it. Bissell cut him short. Like Lord Cochrane, he had much to think about and wished for solitude. Abruptly he took his leave of the Colonel, who was to sail for the Peninsula with his regiment in a week's time, and made his way to the coachhouse where he had left Stella. He found her in the company of the manservant Davie, who had brought a bowl of water for her. She gave her usual half-bark and little jump of pleasure at his return. He presented Davie with his thanks and a shilling and with Stella on lead made his way out of Palace Yard into the street.

The sky of late afternoon was overcast above the thin pall of London smoke, darkening the green of the trees and grass in the Park to which they turned their steps. The pervasive gloom matched Bissell's mood. There were few people walking in the Park and when he found a seat on a fallen treetrunk he was as nearly solitary as a man might be in the heart of London, though from time to time a chaise or carriage trundled along the broad track that ran a pistol-shot away. He released Stella from her lead and sent her off on the 'independent cruise' she expected; suddenly remembering, as he watched the small brown shape speeding away across the turf, the day on Woolwich Common when her upsetting of a military parade had led to his meeting with Kathy. But Kathy did not enter his thoughts for more than a moment, for the fate of Thomas Cochrane occupied the foreground of his mind.

Admiral Lord Gambier's triumph, and Captain Lord Cochrane's consequent downfall, had come as no great surprise; during the past week Bissell had been struggling to keep alive his hopes in the face of a growing conviction that the forces mustered against Cochrane were too strong for him. The verdict had come as a shock all the same, with its overwhelming proof that truth could be suppressed whenever Government or Admiralty wished it to be. His rage smouldered like a fire unable to blaze for lack of draught. It was not so much the Admiral's escape from well-deserved censure that angered him as the unmerited penalty that had fallen upon a naval officer who deserved well of his country if ever a man did. For a wild second or two he entertained the notion of standing on London Bridge and shouting the truth, gathering a mob that would march with him in the name of justice and smash the Admiralty windows. He dismissed the idea with a wry grin at his own folly; he was not the man for that, nor would it do any good.

Stella came racing back, panting, and asked for his approbation. He stroked her head absently, feeling (as always) oddly soothed by this evidence of her attachment to him. Injustice, he reflected, there must always be while men held conflicting loyalties. The admirals and captains who had whitewashed Gambier probably did so out of loyalty to their naval hierarchy, deeming the smothering of Truth a small price to pay for the preservation of the Navy's reputation. But that didn't alter the galling fact that the man who had done all his duty and more was down, while the man who had neglected his was up.

An open chaise passed along the track carrying a naval officer and his lady, and a level ray from the sinking sun, piercing the clouds, set the man's two epaulettes twinkling. Bissell was reminded of his promotion and promised command; but he could take no pleasure in them now. It was shameful, it seemed to him, that he should gain a step in rank and a ship while Cochrane lost *Impérieuse* and all hope of advancement in the Navy.

He was abstractedly caressing the angle below Stella's jaw – it seemed to give her particular pleasure – when he felt the dog stiffen and cock her head. A carriage, proceeding in the opposite direction to the chaise, had come along the track and was passing away from him at a trot. Stella gave one short excited bark and was off like an arrow after the carriage. Bissell sprang to his feet. She had never done such a thing before.

'Heel, Stella!' he yelled after her.

But Stella was prancing alongside the chaise, barking frenziedly at the carriage window. Bissell began to run, noting as he did so that the carriage had stopped. A man got out, a small spare man very neatly dressed in grey, and seemed to speak a word to Stella, who at once sat down at his feet and gazed up at his face as she had done on board *Brunswick*. It was Doctor James Molloy. A stouter gentleman in a green coat was descending from the carriage as Bissell came up; he recognised Kathy's 'honorary uncle', Mr Tierney.

'Mr Bissell, this meeting is most fortunate,' Molloy said, gripping his hand briefly. 'We have been vainly seeking you.'

'We were in Cloak Lane this minute,' added Mr Tierney as they shook hands. 'The good woman there knew nothing of your whereabouts.'

'I've removed to Hay's Mews,' Bissell said.

'The fling of a stone from here,' said the Doctor, looking at his friend.

Bissell glanced from one to the other, aware of tension. Molloy's jaw was tightly set, Mr Tierney's ususally cheerful face wore a curious expression between apprehensiveness and resolution. Both men had something the air of desperados.

'You gentlemen have business with me?' he asked.

'Y-yes – yes, indeed,' Tierney said hesitantly.

'Urgent business,' he added more firmly.

'And private,' said Molloy.

'To my lodging, then, with your leave.' Bissell picked Stella up. 'If we leave by Stanhope Gate –'

'I know it,' Molloy cut in, hustling them into the carriage; he spoke quickly to the coachman on the box. 'South Street, then turn right into Hay's Mews.'

The carriage wheeled about on the turf and headed back along the way it had come. Its occupants were at first silent, Stella sitting on the floor with her eyes on the Doctor's frowning face and Bissell glancing curiously at his companions. Mr Tierney apparently decided it was incumbent on him to make conversation.

'I – ah – must congratulate you, sir, on your heroic behaviour in the Aix Roads,' he said. 'Sure I am that the newspapers didn't tell the half of it.'

Bissell repressed the answer that sprang to his lips. 'Thank you, sir,' he said sombrely. 'I'm but now from Lord Cochrane's house. I learned there that Admiral Lord Gambier has been acquitted by the court-martial.'

Mr Tierney nodded. 'As we all expected.' He saw the expression on the lieutenant's face. 'But you don't agree with the verdict?'

'No.'

There was a finality about the harsh monosyllable that decided Mr Tierney not to press the matter further and they finished the rest of the short journey without further speech. Bissell's withered landlady showed them into the little sitting-room of the Hay's Mews lodging and left them. Doctor Molloy brusquely cut short an invitation to take a glass of sherry and declined to sit down.

'This case requires instant action, in my opinion,' he announced. 'You, Bissell, are a man of action. We'll waste neither words nor time.'

'One moment, James,' Mr Tierney remonstrated nervously. 'Should we not first –'

'You must know,' continued the Doctor, ignoring the interruption, 'that I've lately been in attendance at Bryanstone Square as a medical specialist. Sam Tierney here persuaded Miss Simpson to see me – which, my reputation being what it is, she could hardly refuse. I paid three visits.'

He had begun to pace up and down with short quick steps. Stella had seated herself where she could follow his every movement with her eyes.

'My third and last visit was this afternoon. I used it to deliver an honest diagnosis. I was bidden to begone and not come back.' He halted in front of Bissell. 'Sir, there's a very sick woman in that house.'

'Miss Simpson is seriously ill?' queried Bissell as he paused impressively.

'Miss Honoria Simpson has the gout, sir – podagra. It gives her intermittent pain which I have been able to relieve by administering colchicum. Otherwise there is nothing whatever wrong with her except advanced hypochondria, and so I told her this afternoon. Hence my dismissal.' Doctor Molloy resumed his pacing. ''Tis her niece that's the sick woman, sir. I find Miss Corbett Barnes – ' he waved aside an anxious interjection from Bissell – 'I find her pale, listless, careworn, deteriorating both physically and mentally. Her ailment is devotion to a tyrannical old woman who's been toadied into hypochondria by criminal fools like Arbuthnot. Devotion, do I say? 'Tis self-immolation in an advanced stage. The girl does nothing all day but run up and down stairs at the orders of her aunt.'

'She reads, James,' Mr Tierney ventured.

'Aye – I've noted it. A great blue leather-bound book filled with her own handwriting, and that's all. But read or not, Sam, she's at the end of her tether. A day or two more and she'll be fit for Bedlam – I know the signs and I'm telling you.'

'There's some remedy for this, surely.' Bissell's voice was harsh with anxiety. 'You claim to be an expert in such matters, Doctor Molloy. Can't you –'

'I am an expert, sir, and I know the remedy. I've tried suasion and argument in vain – she's reached the stage of affective obsession, the *idée fixe* as the French professors are calling it. A brick wall would be more responsive to reason. There's but one way to save her.' The Doctor turned to face Bissell. 'She must be got out of that house, at once and forever – by force, if necessary.'

'I hardly think that force,' began Mr Tierney in a fluster, and was again ignored.

'Kidnapped, run away with, anything,' Molloy went on forcibly. 'Her reason's at stake, maybe her life. I can do nothing. Tierney can do nothing.' His piercing grey eyes bored into Bissell's. 'Hence our search for you. Tierney tells me you have a long-standing affection for this lady. You are at least not unknown to her, a friend. You're not afraid to take risks. Would you risk something to save Kathy Barnes from Bedlam, Mr Bissell?'

'Yes. But –'

'Then go to Bryanstone Square this minute. Take my carriage. You're big enough and strong enough to carry her off – do so. Get to Blount's livery stables, hire a fast chaise-and-pair and away with you over the Border. Marry her. You'll find –'

Bissell ceased to hear him. For one mad moment he saw himself playing this primitive part, overbearing Kathy's protests, taking his coveted prize by assault. It passed in a flash. He knew, only too well, that he was not the man to play that part.

' – you can take my word for it that she's in no state to sustain a long siege,' the Doctor was saying. 'Once you have her safe in the –'

'No!' Bissell cut him short harshly. 'You're on the wrong tack, Doctor. Your remedy may be sound but you'll need another man to make it work.' He looked at Tierney. 'She reads only in that blue leather book of hers. He carries her picture wherever he goes.'

'Cochrane?' Mr Tierney exclaimed. 'But he's – after this court-martial –'

'What the devil does that matter when her happiness is at stake?' Bissell roared at him; he swung round and gripped the Doctor's arm. 'Drive straight to Number One Palace Yard. Lord Cochrane's there. Tell him precisely what you've just told me.' He was hustling both men towards the door as he spoke. 'You'll find you've no need to say more.'

At the front door Molloy turned. 'You're sure?' he said.

'This time,' said Bissell with confidence, 'you can't fail.'

He watched the Doctor urge his reluctant and plainly uneasy companion into the carriage. The driver touched up his horses. As the carriage rolled away Stella, watching beside her master, gave a small whine and Bissell heaved a large sigh. The man looked down at the dog with a rueful smile. But for Stella –

'Come along, miss,' he said. 'You'll be wanting your supper.'

3

Bissell and Stella stood on the wooden platform of a warehouse that fronted the Common Hard, viewing Portsmouth Harbour. From this slight elevation they overlooked the quay with its long border of boats and small craft, the mass of vessels moored further out, and the three 74's at the buoys over on the Gosport side. Bissell was employing his telescope, Stella her eyes and nose.

A south-easterly breeze was blowing up Spithead, ruffling the grey water and setting the ships large and small tugging at their cables as if they were as impatient to be away to sea as William Bissell. His glass settled on one of the smaller vessels, flush-decked and two-masted, four yards on each mast; a broad white line ran along her hull and above the line was the row of square gunports, eight of them.

'That's her,' he said aloud, careless of grammar; Stella looked up at him inquiringly. 'His Majesty's brig-sloop *Savage*, sixteen guns,' he added. 'Think she'll do for us, Stella?'

Stella cocked one ear and twisted her head sideways in her eagerness to understand him. He bent to stroke her and then straightened up for another look at his new command. She mounted 6-pounders; complement, 70 men and boys; reasonable in a seaway by the look of her lines. With an extra tackle rigged to the spanker boom the after-deck might give room for a pair of Congreve rocket-frames. A little ship – but his own. She'd do.

In the breast-pocket of his uniform was his commission; he was on his way to read himself in. The same pocket held a letter, received before he left London for Portsmouth. But there was no little lace-edged handkerchief there now. The letter was from Mr Samuel Tierney, and contained the news that Captain Lord Cochrane and Miss Katherine Corbett Barnes had been married at Annan in Scotland.

The somewhat melancholy satisfaction this news had given him was no longer melancholy, he found as he gazed across a quarter-of-a-mile of water at the brig-sloop. A chapter was closed, a new one beginning.

'Come!' he said to Stella, and they went down the platform steps to the quay.

Bissell beckoned to the boy who had his sea-chest on a barrow and led the way to the quay's edge where a big waterman was wiping the thwarts of his wherry.

'I want to be put on board *Savage*, brig-sloop,' he said.

'Aye.' The man glanced at Bissell's epaulette. 'Captain, sir?'

'Yes.'

Bissell gave the boy a shilling, the waterman stowed his dunnage in the bows and cast off his painter.

'On board with you,' Bissell said to Stella.

She jumped into the boat and settled herself below the stern thwart; her master stepped in after her and the wherry shoved off.

'Nice little dawg that, sir,' said the waterman, dipping his oars. 'Knows her dooty, seemingly.'

'She knows more than that,' said Bissell.